# WINTERING

## SECOND EDITION

### BY

## WILLIAM DURBIN

Raven PRODUCTIONS, INC.
PO Box 188, Ely, Minnesota • 218-365-3375 • www.ravenwords.com

Text © 1999 and 2009 by William Durbin

Cover illustration by Matthew Archambault
Map by Virginia Norey

# WINTERING
## 2nd edition
Published October, 2009 by
## Raven Productions, Inc.
P.O. Box 188, Ely, MN 55731

218-365-3375

www.ravenwords.com

First edition published by Delacorte Press®, a division of Random House, Inc.
February, 1999

Library of Congress Cataloging-in-Publication Data

Durbin, William, 1951

Wintering / by William Durbin; [cover illustration by Matthew Archambault; map by
Virginia Norey]. -- 2nd ed.

p. em.

Sequel to: The broken blade.

Summary: In 1801, fourteen-year old Pierre returns to work for the North West Fur
Company and makes the long and difficult journey to a winter camp, where he learns
from both the other voyageurs and from the Ojibwa Indians whose land they share.

ISBN 978-0-9801045-9-2 (softcover: alk. paper)

[1. Fur traders--Fiction. 2. Canada--History--1763-1867--Fiction. 3. Ojibwa Indians--
Fiction. 4. Indians of North America--Canada--Fiction.] I. Archambault, Matthew. II.
Norey, Virginai. III. Title.

PZ7.D9323Wi 2009

[Fic]--dc22

200903833

Printed in Minnesota
United States of America
Sentinel Printing, St. Cloud, MN
10 9 8 7 6 5 4 3 2          092009

*To my daughter Jessica,*

*a student of history without equal.*

I would like to thank Ms. Johnnie Hyde, editor, canoe guide, and wildland firefighter, for supporting the re-publication of this book. Johnnie's knowledge of the north woods was extremely helpful. Special thanks is also due to Denise K. Lajimodiere, a member of the Turtle Mountain Band of Chippewa, who clarified some of the Ojibwe language and cultural references; Wendy Lamb, who edited the original Delacorte Press edition; my agent, Barbara Markowitz, who discovered the beauty of the canoe country as a young girl; the staffs of the Minnesota Historical Society, the Northeast Minnesota Historical Society, Voyageurs National Park, Grand Portage Monument, and the Hibbing Public Library; Sherry Johnson; Shelly Ceglar; Judy Lawrence Kovarik; and my ever-supportive and growing family: Barbara, Jessica, Reid, Darren, Autumn, Linden, Olive, and Abigail.

Finally, I would like to recognize the support of the students, teachers, and librarians throughout the Great Lakes region who continue to study ***Wintering*** and ***The Broken Blade*** as a part of their social studies and English classes. All of you have helped make the re-publication of this novel possible.

# *FOREWORD*

***Wintering*** continues the story of a young voyageur named Pierre La Page, begun in ***The Broken Blade***. That first book is set in 1800 and follows Pierre on a twelve-hundred mile canoe trip from his home in Montréal to Grand Portage, on the northwestern shore of Lake Superior.

The voyageurs were travel-hardened canoe men who transported trade goods and furs along a four-thousand mile waterway that extended from Montréal to the Pacific Ocean. They paddled fourteen to sixteen hours each day and carried loads of nearly two hundred pounds over many miles of rugged portages, the trails around rapids and between lakes. Stopping for only two meals daily and sleeping under their overturned canoes at night, the voyageurs lived hard and often died young. Storytelling, singing, and smoking small clay pipes provided the men with their only relief from the backbreaking labor.

***Wintering*** begins at Grand Portage in the summer of 1801, the year that saw the largest rendezvous, or meeting, in the history of the North West Company, which was Pierre's employer. Thanks to European fashion trends, the fur trade had become a multi-million dollar industry, equivalent to multi-billion dollar businesses today. No well-dressed man went out without a beaver hat, and no fine lady would be seen in public without a bit of fur trim on her coat or dress. With huge fortunes to be made, the Hudson's Bay Company and the newly formed XY Company were both pushing into territory controlled by the North West Company. In response, the

North West called its partners together in the summer of 1801 to plan a strategy for maintaining its share of the trade.

**Wintering** traces Pierre's journey into the wilderness beyond Lake Superior during this dramatic year, along what is today the border between Canada and the United States, and part of the Boundary Waters Canoe Area Wilderness in Minnesota and Quetico Provincial Park in Ontario. The story follows Pierre through his first winter in the North, living on the shore of Lake Vermilion near an Ojibwe village. In becoming an *hivernant*, or winterer, Pierre discovers much about himself and about the native people of the lake country.

William Durbin
Lake Vermilion
September 2009

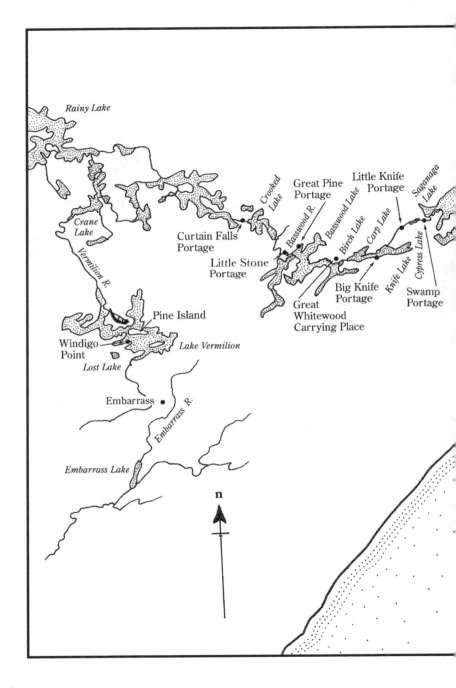

Rainy Lake

Crooked Lake

Great Pine Portage

Little Knife Portage

Saganaga Lake

Crane Lake

Curtain Falls Portage

Basswood R.

Basswood Lake

Birch Lake

Carp Lake

Vermilion R.

Little Stone Portage

Big Knife Portage

Knife Lake

Cypress Lake

Swamp Portage

Great Whitewood Carrying Place

Pine Island

Windigo Point

Lake Vermilion

Lost Lake

Embarrass

Embarrass R.

Embarrass Lake

n

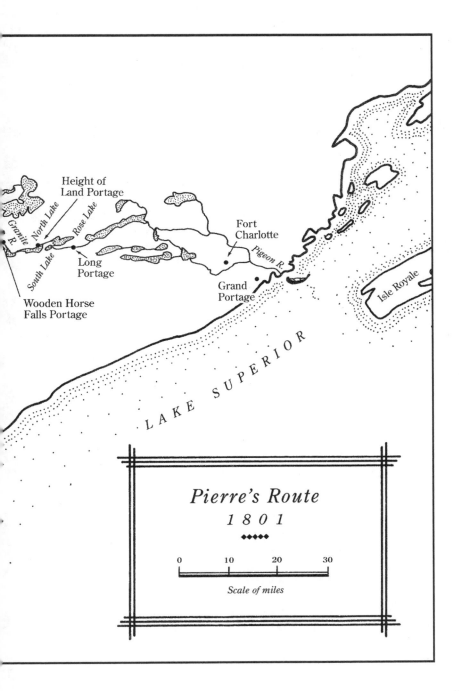

Height of
Land Portage

Granite R.

North Lake

Rose Lake

South Lake

Long
Portage

Wooden Horse
Falls Portage

Fort
Charlotte

Pigeon R.

Grand
Portage

Isle Royale

LAKE SUPERIOR

*Pierre's Route*

*1 8 0 1*

♦♦♦♦♦

0      10      20      30

*Scale of miles*

# Chapter One

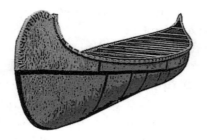

# Bear for Breakfast

"Breakfast off the port bow," Beloît called out. Pierre La Page, who was half asleep, lurched forward at the sudden shout. He rested his paddle blade on the gunwale of the north canoe and looked up.

"Paddle, you fools!" the bowman, Jean Beloît, yelled.

Suddenly the crewmen in all four canoes were pulling hard for the near shore.

Pierre was sick of paddling. The four-canoe brigade had started up the Pigeon River at 4 a.m., when the sun was only a faint glimmer in the pines, yet they still hadn't stopped for breakfast. This was Pierre's second summer with the North West Company, and though he was becoming a skilled canoeman, he was travel weary this morning. He had paddled and portaged a thousand miles since he'd left Montréal last May.

It was July now, and only two days ago his brigade had carried its huge load of trade goods over the legendary nine-mile trail at Grand Portage. He'd made four trips without complaint, carrying two ninety-pound packs up the trail and returning with an equal weight of bundled furs each time. It had nearly done him in. Pierre could understand why the old timers joked that the North West Company used voyageurs to portage the freight because they couldn't risk laming mules or horses.

"I said paddle!" Beloît yelled, raising his Northwest gun and aiming it over the bow.

Pierre squinted in the harsh light. Beloît was the grossest man Pierre had ever seen. Though most of the voyageurs took pride in their appearance, tying long fringed sashes around their waists and carefully perching their red woolen caps on their heads, Beloît was a picture of neglect. When he wasn't bare chested, his soiled shirt hung loosely over his hips. His sweat-stained cap sagged over his ears, and he refused to wear socks or deerskin leggings like the rest of the crew. Beloît's hair was long and greasy, and his bloodshot eyes were small and black. He wore an evil grin, made worse by the fact that he was missing a front tooth, and the left half of his nose had been bitten off in a fight years ago, leaving only a ragged hole.

Beloît said, "Ship your paddles," and the men held their paddles still as the canoe went into a silent glide.

When Pierre saw the bear, he felt sorry for it. Shooting an animal in the water wasn't sporting. Pierre's father told him that a true hunter always gave his game a fair chance.

Since the bear was only twenty yards from shore and swimming fast, Pierre thought it might escape. Then he heard the hammer click back on Beloît's gun. "Come on, sweet Tillie," Beloît whispered, talking to his gun as he always did just before he shot.

In the powder flash and roar that followed, a pair of mallards rose from a reed bed on the far shore. The crewmen cheered as the bear went limp in the water. Beloît shouted his favorite phrase, "*Je suis l'homme!*" ("I am the man!") He waved his gun high overhead in a victory salute.

From his narrow seat in the canoe, Pierre stared at the

bear. As it floated face down in the water, blood pooled at its shoulder and paled to a misty pink, spreading outward into the clear waters of Mountain Lake. The bear smelled as bad as Pierre's dog, Pepper, did after he'd waded into a swamp back home.

"Roast bear for breakfast," Beloît grinned, showing his yellow teeth as he slipped a leather cord around the bear's foreleg and tied the loose end around his wrist. "Let's tow her to shore, *mesdemoiselles.*"

The steersman in Pierre's canoe, a giant fellow whom the voyageurs called La Petite, cursed at Beloît and said, "Watch who you're calling girls, pretty boy," but Beloît only laughed harder.

When the canoe floated into the shallows, Beloît stepped out into the knee-deep water.

"You taking a bath?" yelled the gray-haired cook, André Bellegarde.

"Once a year is plenty," Beloît said, wrapping another turn of the cord around his wrist. "Get your skinning knife ready, Bellegarde."

Then, as Beloît jerked the carcass toward shore, the bear lifted his head out of the water. With a gurgling snort and a horrifying growl, the bear leaped up.

"No!" Beloît yelled, pulling on the leather cord. He tried to hold the bear back as it ran up the bank. "Noooo!!" he yelled a second time, planting his moccasins against a rock.

The crew stared openmouthed as the line tightened and Beloît flew forward. He landed on his belly, and the bear dragged him toward the trees. Just when it looked as if the bowman were going to disappear into the woods, his head smacked into a huge red pine and the cord snapped.

Beloît lay flat on his stomach. He didn't even move when a green pine cone fell from the tree and hit his head. The crewmen stared silently. He's dead! Pierre thought.

When Beloît finally moaned and rolled over, all four canoes rocked with the men's laughter. His face was caked with mud and blood, and the front of his shirt was covered with pine needles. A hunk of moss stuck to his beard, and his dirty red cap tilted to one side.

"You alive, Greenbeard?" Bellegarde chuckled.

Beloît, still dazed, grabbed the hunk of moss and dirt hanging on his chest. "Greenbeard, eh? Take this and flavor your soup."

As the moss flew over Bellegarde's head and splashed into the lake, the crew had another good laugh.

Since it was already midmorning, the voyageurs moored their canoes in the shallows and stepped ashore for their usual breakfast of boiled corn and pork fat. Pierre was amazed that the voyageurs could paddle twelve to sixteen hours a day on only two meals. They rose well before dawn and paddled three or four hours before they stopped for breakfast.

The mornings were tough on Pierre. At fourteen, he was always hungry. He'd added three inches and twenty pounds to his frame over the past winter, and he could never get enough to eat. He was already five feet, eight inches—taller than the average voyageur—and his canoe mates constantly teased him about his appetite. They also joked about his blonde hair and blue eyes, since nearly all the voyageurs were dark. "We'll have to get Blondie his own canoe if he grows any more," La Petite said as they waded toward shore.

"No," the weasel-eyed cook, Bellegarde, paused to finger the white claw marks on his cheek, left by a grizzly years ago. "We'll just shorten his legs with my meat saw." Bellegarde roared at his own joke.

Pierre didn't laugh. He missed his old canoe mate, Charles La Londe. La Londe had been a good-natured fellow who walked with a light step and a smile. He was famous for his shoulder-length white hair, and no matter how dark or windy the day, he encouraged his crew, unlike Bellegarde and Beloît, who lived to torture and tease. In Pierre's first days as a middle man last spring, his clumsy paddling had left his hands blistered and bloody. Yet La Londe had gone out of his way to teach him the proper rhythm and pace for an all-day paddle. "You've got to trick the work by dreaming of grander things," he'd said.

Pierre often thought back to the terrible day when La Londe had drowned in the French River rapids. La Londe had saved his entire crew by jumping onto a rock and freeing their bow, just as an oncoming canoe swept by. But he'd slipped into the water. The only trace they found of his body was his cap and a single feather. Why did it have to be him? Pierre wondered, thinking back to the paddle blade cross they'd placed above the river to honor the passing of their friend.

As Bellegarde ladled a portion of corn soup onto Pierre's tin plate, Pierre almost wished Beloît had killed the bear. He was starving.

Pierre knew that the men hated Beloît, but he thought someone would at least offer to inspect his wounds. However, they wolfed down their breakfast as if nothing unusual had happened. But when they sat back and lit their pipes, the teasing began.

Bellegarde said, "I can't believe that weak-kneed scoundrel let two days of good meat run off into the woods without even putting up a struggle."

La Petite chuckled, "No bear could best a real bowman."

For once Beloît was speechless. Hoping for sympathy, he'd refused to wash his face or brush off his clothes, but the men were still teasing him long after they'd packed away their tobacco pouches and boarded their canoes.

# Chapter Two

# The Rendezvous

The men pulled on their paddles, falling into the stroke-a-second pace they would hold all day. Portages and pipe stops provided the only break in their routine. The portages were even more brutal than the paddling, so Pierre looked forward to the pipe stops every couple of hours. Though Pierre didn't smoke, he enjoyed the rest. When the time came, the men set down their paddles and let the canoes drift. They lit their little clay pipes and rested with their backs propped against the thwarts or the parcels of trade goods, sharing stories and jokes for ten to fifteen minutes.

The previous summer, during his first trip as a voyageur, Pierre had unwisely counted his paddle strokes early in the trip. After multiplying an hour's paddling by the fifteen hours they'd canoed that day, Pierre found that he'd taken 57,000 strokes. Knowing the huge number made his job twice as hard. In fact, it was only after La Londe convinced him to think of other things while he was paddling that his work became tolerable.

Pierre was still getting used to his north canoe. Only twenty-five feet long, it was trimmer than the big freight canoes his brigade had paddled from Montréal to Grand Portage. Their craft carried the steersman, La Petite; the bowman, Beloît; Pierre and three other middlemen who sat amidships and did the bulk of the paddling. The three thousand pounds of merchandise stored between the seats of the canoe included kettles, axe heads, knives, guns, tobacco, cloth, ribbon, beads, and food, all packed in ninety-pound bales for portaging. The freight also included two wooden kegs, one filled with gunpowder and another with sugar, and ten kegs of rum.

Pierre was excited about his first trip into the vast wilderness that lay north of Lake Superior. Once they turned off the main supply route and headed for their wintering post, they would be paddling through territory that had been seen by only a handful of white men. His father, Charles La Page, had been a North West steersman for most of his life, and he'd often told Pierre stories about the North. He'd given Pierre advice last May, the morning his brigade departed from his home in Lachine. "Never forget that you're a guest in the North," he said as Pierre hugged his mother one last time. "It's *Anishinaabe* country, and our travel and trading couldn't happen without their help."

Pierre liked the sound of the word *"Anishinaabe."* Most people called the north woods tribes Chippewa or Ojibway, which were different English versions of the same word. But Pierre's father knew the native language well enough to use the name the Indians called themselves. After many winters trading in the north, Father had just been promoted to clerk of the North West Company depot in Lachine. He hated to give up his voyaging life, but Mother had talked him into accepting the position.

"Just think how nice it will be to rest from all your voyaging," Mother said. "And for once you can see one of your children grow up." She nodded toward Pierre's little sister, Claire, asleep under the feather quilt in her cradle.

As the afternoon breeze picked up, La Petite started a song. *"En roulant ma boule, roulant,"* his big baritone voice boomed over the blue water. The voyageurs pulled hard on their paddles and joined in at the chorus. Singing made the days go faster, and steersmen with good voices commanded extra pay.

As Pierre paddled, his mind reeled with images of last week's rendezvous back at Grand Portage. Pierre's brigade had arrived on July 1, 1801, just in time to see the largest gathering of North West Company officials in the history of the territory. Including the Montréalers from back east and the wintering partners from the far north, three thousand voyageurs and Ojibwe were present for the week long celebration.

After the long paddle from Montréal, the fort at Grand Portage was a welcome sight to Pierre. It was the largest and most famous fur depot in the Northwest Territory. A long wharf led to a gate and a palisade of vertical logs. Inside, the courtyard contained sixteen squared-timber buildings, including the Great Hall, the cook shack, warehouses, offices, and living quarters for the company partners and clerks, some of whom lived there year round.

Every brigade stopped at Grand Portage for at least a brief rendezvous, or meeting. The crewmen celebrated, while the commanders met with company officials, tallied their supplies, and planned the final details of their expeditions. The previous summer Pierre had paddled home to Montréal after the rendezvous, but this year he was headed north to spend the winter. Now there were only 150 miles and two dozen portages between him and the trading post where he would winter over. After paddling from Grand Portage to Crane Lake, his brigade would split into two groups. One party would travel north to Quetico Lake while the other headed south to Lake Vermilion. Each group would build a trading post, exchange trade goods for furs with the Indians throughout the winter, and return to Crane Lake with the bundles of pelts as soon as the ice was off the lakes in the spring.

Shortly after Pierre had arrived at Grand Portage, he was startled by a volley of gun shots and a deafening "Hurrah!"

He sprinted over to La Petite and asked, "What's going on?"

"Here comes the Premier," La Petite hollered over the raucous crowd of voyageurs and Indians. Powder smoke drifted out across Portage Bay. Dogs barked up and down the shore.

"Who?" Pierre asked, squinting into the sun.

"Simon McTavish." La Petite leaned closer. "Premier is just his nickname. He's the head of the whole North West Company. Every official from here to Athabasca answers to him."

Father often mentioned McTavish's name, but no one Pierre knew had ever seen him.

"He's come from a meeting in London," La Petite continued. "He's here to rally us for a big push this season. They say heads will roll if that new XY Company takes over any more of our trade routes."

"I thought our only competition was the Hudson's Bay Company?" Pierre asked.

"It's both," La Petite stared toward the pier. "With the XY men and the border dispute working against us down here, and the Hudson's Bay men pushing down from the north, they're afraid we might get squeezed out. Our company's stock is worth half of what it was five years ago. Look! Here he comes!"

The cheers were even louder now. Four men hoisted McTavish onto their shoulders and carried him through the gates of the fort. "McTavish loves a show," La Petite said. "That's how he always comes ashore."

The next morning another famous Nor'wester, John McDonald, a towering Scotsman, marched through the fort gates with a long sword buckled at his waist. Pierre heard a man whisper, "You'll not find a more dangerous man on this earth. He'd sooner run you through with his sword than look at you."

As Pierre studied the bold characters arriving for the rendezvous, he was disappointed in his own commander, William McHenry. Tall and pale, McHenry wore a blue waist coat, a flat-topped hat, and a look of perpetual confusion. On their trip from Montréal he'd spent his evenings alone in his tent, reading his books or writing in his journal. McHenry left the daily management of the crew to La Petite or Maurice Blondeau, the most experienced voyageurs.

Soon after Pierre arrived at Grand Portage, he decided to walk to the Ojibwe camp and visit Makwa, the local chief. The previous summer, Jacques Charbonneau had introduced Pierre to Makwa and his family. Though Makwa was a colorful fellow, Pierre was mainly interested in seeing his dark-eyed daughter, Kennewah. A year had passed since he had last visited her village, yet the picture of her shy smile, her shining black hair, and her soft doeskin dress was as clear in Pierre's mind as if he had seen her yesterday.

When Pierre told La Petite he was going up to the village, Beloît overheard. "So is little La Page going to see his *mademoiselle*?" Beloît's black eyes glittered as he wiped his scarred nose with the back of his dirty hand. "What was her name again? Many Kisses?"

When Pierre blushed, Beloît laughed.

"Her name is Kennewah," Pierre said, hurrying up the trail. How he hated the ugly bowman!

"That's what I said," Beloît hollered after him, "Kennewah Many Kisses." He roared so loudly that Pierre was sure every man in Grand Portage heard his cackle.

Pierre hurried along the river path that divided the voyageurs into two camps—the pork eaters and the *hivernants*. The pork eaters were men who paddled from

Montréal to Grand Portage and never ventured further north. They slept under their canoes just like they did on the trail. The *hivernants* wintered in the North. They looked with disdain on the pork eaters and were privileged to lodge in tents. Fights were common between the two groups. Pierre would remain a pork eater until he hiked over the Grand Portage and paddled as far as the Height of Land, the point where the rivers began flowing north.

East of the voyageur encampment lay the canoe works. Here Pierre had first met Chief Makwa. He dressed outrageously in bright shirts and waist coats and ostrich feathers, but he treated his friends with courtesy.

Each year the Ojibwe who lived near the fort built about seventy canoes for the North West Company. Along the shore, boats stood in various stages of completion as the workers shaped the birchbark between stakes pounded into the ground, stitched the bark with spruce root, and sealed the seams with pitch. Pierre approached two Ojibwe men who were painting the gunwales of a north canoe in alternate swatches of green, red, and white. "Where can I find Makwa?" he asked.

They both shook their heads and said, "*Nibowin.*" Pierre asked about Kennewah, but they repeated, "*Nibowin.*"

Did "*nibowin*" mean they didn't know French? Pierre walked up to the village. He found Makwa's wigwam, but no one was home. After waiting all winter to see Kennewah again, he would have to wait yet another day.

Though he and Kennewah had spent only a short time together, she'd become as special to him as his friend Celeste, back in Lachine. Celeste was the daughter of Dr. Guilliard, and she and Pierre had attended the same school. She was the only person he'd ever confided in about his dream of attending college someday. When Pierre reenrolled as a voyageur last spring, they'd even joked about getting married.

Pierre would never forget the moment. He and Celeste were walking along the bank of the St. Lawrence, enjoying the first real warmth of the season. An early brigade was readying for departure, and just ahead four men were carrying a thirty-six-foot Montréal canoe toward the water.

"If I were Madame La Page," Celeste teased, "could I ride with you in your canoe?"

"Why of course, *mademoiselle*," he laughed. "I would throw a parcel of trade goods into the river and make a special seat just for you."

"How gallant of you, *monsieur*." Celeste offered Pierre her hand and curtsied.

"For your Ladyship, nothing would be too good." Pierre continued the game by bowing low and kissing the back of her wrist. "And each night I would save you the sweetest piece of pork fat from my corn soup."

Celeste wrinkled her nose. "Pork fat? We mustn't become too familiar, *Monsieur* La Page." Her blue eyes danced mischievously as she pulled back her hand and tossed her white shawl over her shoulder. Her fine black hair, which was normally gathered into a tight braid, hung loosely down her back that day.

Though the joking was fun, it made him feel sad. Since his family were paupers compared to the Guilliards, he knew that no matter how much he and Celeste liked each other, their talk of marriage must remain a joke. Unless, by some miracle, he could earn enough money to complete his education and raise his station in life, there was no hope for him to marry Celeste.

So his trip this summer was tied to a twofold dream. But his feelings for Kennewah complicated the picture. He'd never said a word to Celeste about her. If Kennewah was just a friend, Pierre should have been honest and told Celeste about her. He could have said, "Did I tell you about the nice Ojibwe girl I met at Grand Portage?" Yet he hadn't.

Now that Pierre was about to meet Kennewah again, he could admit the reason for his hesitancy. He would never be sure of his feelings for Celeste until he spoke with Kennewah one more time.

When he returned to the voyageur camp, La Petite approached Pierre and winked. "How was Kennewah?"

"I couldn't find her," Pierre said. "I asked two fellows about her, but they couldn't speak French. They kept saying *nibowin.*"

La Petite shrugged. "We'll be here the rest of the week; you'll have time to …"

"Did you say *nibowin*?" Bellegarde interrupted.

Pierre nodded.

Touching his bear claw necklace, Bellegarde said, "That's too bad, son."

"What do you mean?"

"*Nibowin* means dead."

"No!" Pierre cried. He couldn't even imagine such a thing. There was so much he needed to say to Kennewah, and to ask her.

"I was afraid of that," La Petite said. "The men were saying that smallpox hit hard here last winter. Some of the villages lost half their people."

"*Nibowin*?" Pierre repeated. He thought of Kennewah's dark eyes and ebony hair … her innocence … her gentle humor …

Bellegarde nodded. "I'm sorry, son. I know it's hard, but lots of these Indians live short lives."

La Petite patted Pierre on the shoulder. "The deck's stacked against them. If smallpox doesn't do 'em in, consumption, diphtheria, and syphilis are waiting their turn. They've got no way to fight the white man's diseases."

Pierre walked back to the Ojibwe village, hoping that he had misunderstood. Bellegarde came along to interpret. They soon found a nephew of Makwa's, who confirmed that the worst had happened. "The only member of

Makwa's family that survived was the old grandmother," the nephew explained through Bellegard. "And after she prepared the last body for the gravehouse—it was her little grandson Kewatin—she cut off her hair and walked into the woods to die."

His words sounded cold and matter-of-fact. When so many died, Pierre supposed, funerals became commonplace.

When the nephew finished speaking, he touched the bearclaw necklace around Bellegarde's neck and pointed to the scars on the cook's face. Bellegarde smiled. He was proud of surviving a grizzly bear attack, and he loved to tell the story.

"We was in the foothills of the Rockies ..." Bellegarde began.

Pierre walked away, feeling a need to be alone. Without any clear destination in mind, he wandered toward Mount Rose, a rocky hill that overlooked the fort. What would he have said to Kennewah? He'd imagined the meeting a hundred times during his long paddle from Montréal, but he'd never gone beyond a simple hello. Did it matter now?

The trail wound back and forth across the south face of the ridge. In places huge piles of slate had fallen off the cliff, and on the steepest part of the trail, little steps were chipped out of the rock for footholds. When Pierre reached the summit his heart was pounding.

He looked out over Portage Bay and past Hat Point to the great lake beyond. To the south was the hillside where he and Kennewah had picked blueberries last summer. They'd met by accident. She was so beautiful that Pierre had been afraid to breathe. In his nervousness he'd tipped over a berry basket, but Kennewah only laughed. Pierre was used to the jeers of the schoolyard and the evil cackling of Beloît, but her laughter was without ridicule or scorn. That was when Pierre smiled, too.

Though Kennewah knew only a little French and he

knew even less Ojibwe, they had spent the whole afternoon together, filling her birch berry baskets, hiking, and laughing …

Laughing, Pierre thought. That was only a summer ago, yet she would never laugh again.

He looked to the north. A dip in the tree line showed the famous Grand Portage gap and the trail that would soon take him deep into the wilderness.

He turned and stared at the miniature men and buildings below. The sun was sinking fast, and beyond the fort, pink-gold light spilled over the water. For the moment it was easy to imagine he was a god, enthroned on a stone mountain, sitting in silent judgment of the world. Though the Great Hall was barely a stone's throw away, in the evening haze it looked as if it were many miles distant.

If only, Pierre thought, I could point a finger and right the wrongs of this world. If only fools like Beloît could be sent to eternal damnation like they deserve, and bright souls like Kennewah and Makwa and La Londe could live to light the world.

Pierre wished he could sit on the mountain forever. It was dark and quiet—a perfect place to be alone and think. He knew the voyageurs would celebrate tonight. Pierre could already hear a fiddle and a flute tuning up for a dance.

Once the fur presses closed down for the day, the two busiest places in Grand Portage were the canteen and the jail. As hard as the voyageurs worked, they played even harder. The *hivernants* were especially rowdy after a long winter in the wilderness, and at least a dozen men were thrown into the stockade every day. It wasn't unusual for a man to squander a month's wages on liquor in a single night. "And the more they spend," La Petite said, "the more likely it is they'll buy themselves a night's lodging in the guardhouse."

While the canoe men celebrated outside the palisades,

the company officials held fancy balls inside the fort. According to Commander McHenry, the Great Hall blazed with dozens of candles, and the norwester celebrated till dawn. Dressed in their best Eastern finery, the company partners and their guests danced Highland flings, quadrilles, reels, and square dances accompanied by violins and bagpipes. Between dances they drank wine and feasted on trout, smoked whitefish, venison, buffalo tongue, beaver tail, and fresh butter.

In the voyageur camp a squeaky fiddle and a sailor's pipe played, while the canoe men danced, sang, and told stories through the night. The background noise of drums, howling dogs, shrieks, and gunshots never distracted them for a moment.

Pierre rubbed his brow at the thought of another all-night party. How could he sort through his feelings surrounded by two thousand crazy men who were drinking themselves into oblivion? Grateful for the peace of the mountain, he sat on a rock still warm from the sun, and looked up at the stars. Why, in a world of violent, crazy men, did someone as gentle as Kennewah have to be the one to die?

# Chapter Three

# The Long Carry

When Pierre got back to the fort late that night, the voyageurs were all talking about a portage that a man in Daniel Harmon's brigade had completed that very afternoon. According to the stories, the fellow Nor'Wester had carried two ninety-pound parcels of trade goods over the nine-mile Grand Portage to Fort Charlotte and returned with two bundles of furs in only four hours.

Beloît declared, "I can't see why anyone would make a fuss over a simple day's work!"

Harmon's men were camped next to McHenry's crew, and they fell silent. One burly voyageur set down the tin cup he was drinking from and stood up. "Are you claiming you could do as well, Beloît?"

"*Je suis l'homme!*" Beloît said, and Harmon's crew laughed at his boldness. "If I was inclined to bust a gut, I could match any of you sissies. But I know a fellow who could double that carry."

"And who might that be?"

Pierre watched La Petite glare at Beloît, but there was no stopping him now. "I'm talking, of course, about my good friend here," Beloît continued, "Monsieur Petite."

"Joseph Jourdain, you say?" the man replied. A

murmur rose from his crewmates. Everyone knew La Petite's reputation.

In a moment the odds were set. It was three to one against La Petite carrying a 360-pound load to Fort Charlotte and back in four hours. To pacify his friend, Beloît declared that twenty Spanish dollars would go to La Petite if he achieved the carry. But even with such a prize, La Petite wagged a finger in Beloît's face, saying, "If you ever enter me in a contest again without asking, I'll feed you to the trout."

The event began at six the following morning. "Work is not so bad if it is finished before the heat of the day," La Petite declared as McHenry and Harmon compared their watches. Beloît and Bellegarde helped La Petite strap on the four packs and adjust the tumpline that stretched across his forehead to help support and balance the load. The crowd cheered as La Petite started up the trail.

Pierre worried about La Petite, for lifting too much could ruin a man. The doctors called it "strangulated hernia," but to Pierre's father it was simply "busting your guts." Pierre's uncle had died that way at only twenty-three, and according to Father, hernias killed more voyageurs than all the whitewater and Indians in the Northwest Territory.

Like all long carries, this one was divided into poses, or short rests. Several dozen people followed La Petite to the first pose, but only Beloit and Pierre and a handful of other friends trailed on from there.

At first it looked like La Petite would make the carry with ease. He skipped the first pose and rested only briefly at the second and third. But as the hill got steeper, his stride shortened, and his breath got quick and shallow.

Sweat soon beaded his forehead, and he was wheezing like an exhausted runner. "You can do it," Pierre called.

At the next pose, La Petite collapsed with his pack straps in place, and the awkward load tipped him onto his side. His shirt was soaked with sweat, and the straps had cut into his shoulders.

Beloît got down on all fours and stuck his scarred nose in La Petite's face. "We're nearly to the flat," he yelled. "The tough part's done." Pierre felt like shouting, "Leave him alone!" but La Petite took up his load again.

When Fort Charlotte was still an hour away, Pierre suddenly realized that the big man would make it. In that instant Pierre saw that the secret to a great carry was the same as the secret of an all-day paddle.

He recalled the advice that La Londe had offered the previous summer. At the time he didn't understand it, but today it made sense. "A tough portage or a hard paddle is the same," La Londe said. "You have to give yourself over to the power of the hill, just as a paddler must lose himself in the rhythm of the waves."

When La Petite arrived back at Grand Portage with 360 pounds of bundled furs, cheers sounded throughout the fort. Pierre knew he'd witnessed an event that would outlive them all. Even before the packs were lifted from La Petite's shoulders, the money was changing hands.

Beloît was counting coins like a greedy child when La Petite suddenly called, "Beloît." For a moment Pierre thought La Petite had injured himself. "Jean Beloît," he repeated, "we are not yet done."

The crowd turned silent as Beloît walked over and stood in front of La Petite. "Turn around," La Petite commanded.

Then La Petite lifted a dusty pack from the ground and hooked it on Beloît's shoulders. He did the same with a second pack. Beloît was silent until La Petite reached for another.

"No," Beloît croaked, as La Petite positioned the third pack on top of the others. He tipped forward and then back. The veins on his temples popped out, and his legs trembled. Everyone was grinning at what would happen next.

When the full weight of the fourth pack hit him, Beloît's legs gave out. The crowd roared as he flew backwards, his eyes wide and his hands clutching at the air. On the ground he wriggled like a turtle trying to right itself.

Only then did La Petite declare, "Now we are done, Brother Jean."

From that day forward things happened fast. Half of the crew who'd arrived with Pierre paddled home to Montréal with parcels of furs, while McHenry gathered together the small group he was taking north. They would be traveling in a four-canoe brigade as far as Crane Lake. From there, two canoes would paddle north to establish a winter trading post on Quetico Lake, while the other two headed south to do the same on Lake Vermilion.

Along with the men Pierre already knew—La Petite, Bellegarde, and Beloît—the commander added two new recruits to his canoe: a young voyageur named Amblé Le Clair, who, like Pierre, would be spending his first winter in the North; and an older fellow, Augustine Delacroix.

Amblé's nickname was Louie, after his middle name, Louis; but since he had a high, squeaky voice and talked so much, the men called him Squeaks or Noise Box. Louie laughed off the teasing, and the men soon discovered that if they teased him too much, he got so excited that he talked even more. Louie claimed to be five feet tall, but Pierre guessed he was closer to four feet, ten inches. Pierre wondered how the little guy would be able to carry two packs over the portages.

The men called Augustine by his full name at all times. Short, thick-chested, and bald, he was old for a voyageur—Pierre guessed he was over fifty—and he kept to himself. When Pierre asked him how long he'd been a voyageur, he spat, "A voyageur I'm not. For forty years I've been a sailor. I've seen every port from Singapore to Cape Horn." He jerked his head toward Lake Superior, "No man can voyage on a pond such as that."

As he strode away, La Petite chuckled. "You'll have to excuse him, Pierre. After all those years at sea, he finally decided to settle down on a farm outside Montréal. But when he came home last spring, his wife had run off with the local butcher. He enrolled with the North West Company the very next day."

"And he's going to winter over?" Pierre asked.

La Petite nodded. "He wants to get as far away from that woman as he possibly can."

Pierre hoped that the old fellow's mood would improve. He couldn't imagine wintering with two ill-tempered characters like Beloît and Augustine.

# Chapter Four

# Height of Land

"**B**e careful, school boy," Beloît said. "That pack weighs a whole lot more than a spelling book."

For a moment the words didn't register in Pierre's mind. He'd been thinking about Kennewah again. Ever since he'd learned that she had died, he could think of little else. Even his brutal carry two days earlier across the Grand Portage had only been a blur. Four times he'd carried his required two packs of trade goods up the trail to Fort Charlotte and returned with two bundles of furs, but his heart wasn't in it.

That day the nine-mile portage had been a dream world, peopled by faces of the dead. Once he saw Makwa standing in the ostrich-plumed hat he loved to wear. The chief looked so real that Pierre had to rub his eyes. Another time Pierre pictured a feast in Makwa's wigwam. Kennewah held her baby brother, Kewatin, on her lap, and as the little boy nibbled on maple candy, he pointed his tiny finger at Pierre and grinned.

"Do you hear me, schoolboy? That's no spelling book." Beloît's voice shocked Pierre back to reality.

"At least I know how to spell more than rum and

tavern," Pierre snapped back. Pierre had learned that Beloît respected people who stood up to him. But when Beloît touched the hilt of his knife, Pierre thought he'd gone too far.

Beloît looked sideways at Pierre with his black eyes shining. Pierre held his breath until Beloît slapped his knee. "If they'd learned me to spell fine words like tavern in school," he laughed, "I might've stayed past the third grade."

"You quit school in third grade?" Pierre asked, struggling to imagine Beloît as a little boy in knee breeches.

"You heard right." Beloît laughed again. "They were so cheap, they kept that school awful cold. One day the sister told me I'd burn in eternal fire if I kept using the Lord's name in vain. So I stood up and said, 'At least I'll be warm there,' and I walked right out the door."

"Stop filling the boy's head with nonsense," La Petite said. "We've got important things to do this afternoon."

"Such as?" Beloît countered.

"Such as baptisms." La Petite winked.

Pierre frowned. What did he mean? He was still tired from the steep, two-thousand-yard Rose Lake portage. Augustine had cursed it as "a path unfit for goats." The old sailor was especially angry because it was his turn to carry one of McHenry's book crates. The commander had two wooden crates filled with books, and they caused a lot of grumbling among the men.

"What do you suppose they mean by baptisms?" Louie asked Pierre.

"Caulk that mouth, Noise Box," Beloît sneered. "We got big plans."

When Louie asked, "What sort of plans?" Beloît tossed him a pack. "Cork it, Squeaks. Plans that will never happen if you don't stop flappin' your lips and start portaging."

Louie shouldered his load and started up the trail at a

trot. Pierre had been amazed at how strong he was for a little guy. McHenry patted Louie on the shoulder and said, "Remember, lad, 'In silence there is a worth that brings no risk.'" Pierre smiled. This quote from Plutarch was a favorite of Sister Anne's, one of his teachers back in Lachine.

As much as Louie talked, he rarely mentioned his past. The only thing that Pierre had learned was that Louie's father had traveled to Paris on a business trip the previous year, and for some reason he had never returned. Louie's Mother and his three little sisters had moved in with his grandparents, but the house was so small that Louie decided to sign on as a voyageur. "Sleeping under a canoe is a lot less crowded than our little house was," he said, "and a lot quieter, too."

"Quieter than spending all day and all night with Beloît?" Pierre asked.

"Without a doubt," Louie said, smiling. Pierre wondered just how difficult Louie's life had been.

After the brigade crossed South Lake, they reached the Height of Land Portage. Pierre's father had often told him about this famous continental divide. Here, rivers to the north flowed all the way to Hudson's Bay, while the waters to the south ran through the Great Lakes and out the St. Lawrence River. Both systems eventually reached the Atlantic Ocean.

The minute they finished their last carry, La Petite called Pierre and Louie to his side. "Gentlemen," he began, "as newcomers entering the waters of the Northwest Territory for the very first time, it is my honor to accept you into a rare corps of men."

Commander McHenry, who was standing off to one side, smiled at the boys. At the same time, a dozen men appeared behind La Petite, carrying muskets.

"Are you ready, Bellegarde?" La Petite asked, as the grimy cook stepped forward, toting a copper kettle filled with lake water. In his free hand he held a cedar bough.

La Petite winked at the voyageurs, who were now crowded around. "Let's get this ceremony started." He turned to Pierre and Louie. "Repeat after me."

Pierre, blushing at all the attention, repeated, "I, Pierre Charles La Page, do solemnly promise ... to never let a new hand pass into the waters of the Northwest ... without first administering this same ceremony which I now attend."

As he and Louie recited their lines, the men all nodded.

"And furthermore," Pierre repeated, blushing brighter, "I swear that I will never kiss another voyageur's wife ... without her permission."

At this point Bellegarde shouted, "Permission or not, you keep your lips off my Rosie, La Page, or I'll skin your hide." At the thought of Pierre romancing Bellegarde's old, toothless wife, the men roared with laughter.

After the noise died down, La Petite asked Pierre and Louie to kneel. Then he dipped the cedar bough in the kettle and sprinkled each boy with a few drops of lake water. "I now declare you *hommes du nord*—men of the north," he said.

The men cheered and threw their hats into the air. Then twelve Northwest guns fired one after another. Before the powder smoke had cleared, Bellegarde appeared with a keg under his arm and a tin cup in his hand.

The whole brigade lined up at the keg, and as soon as their cups were filled, McHenry raised his hand. "Before we all celebrate—and knowing the likes of you, I'm sure it's celebrating that you have on your minds—we must toast these former boys, who now stand before us as men." He lifted his battered tin cup and said, "To Monsieur Pierre La Page and Monsieur Amblé Le Clair—north men for now and ever after."

Though Louie immediately choked down a swig, Pierre hesitated. He recalled the previous summer when, in his haste to prove himself a man, he'd drunk several glasses of rum. It had given him a headache he would never forget, and he hadn't touched a dram since. He swallowed one small taste, trying not to choke on the burning liquid. Then when no one was looking, he poured the rest on the ground.

Most of the men downed their drams in a single gulp and crowded around Bellegarde for a second draught. Though Bellegard offered Pierre a refill, he shook his head.

The voyageurs usually didn't begin their fun till after supper was served and the campfire was blazing. So it was strange to watch the men celebrating so frantically in daylight. But this was true to the character of the canoe men. If there was food, they ate till it was gone; if there was rum, they drank till they emptied the keg. Voyageurs did nothing in moderation. Quick to anger and just as quick to forgive, they lived hard and died young. Only last June Pierre had watched La Petite and Beloît beat each other senseless during supper, then forget their argument before bedtime.

By late afternoon the singing and storytelling was at a fevered pitch. Pierre studied McHenry. Though the commander had taken off his coat in the heat of the day, he still wore his tall, wide-brimmed felt hat. McHenry was sitting beside Maurice Blondeau and listening to Beloît tell a story, or more likely, a lie. McHenry looked more like a pale preacher than a northman. Pierre could imagine him riding off on a nag to deliver a sermon at a country church.

When McHenry retired to his tent a short while later, Pierre turned to La Petite. "The commander doesn't look like he's spent much time in the North," Pierre began.

"McHenry?" La Petite look surprised. "Why he's traveled more miles in the wilderness than any two of us added together! He's only with the North West because he quit the Hudson's Bay Company. He was one of the first white men to cross the Arctic Barrens. He commanded the expedition that ..." La Petite stopped suddenly when a cheer rose from the other side of the fire. "Looks like a little contest. Let's see if it's worth a wager."

Pierre trailed behind, thinking. McHenry a famous Arctic explorer? Surely not.

He wanted to ask more, but La Petite had other things on his mind now. The men were getting ready for a knife throwing contest.

"The first to hit the mark wins the pot," Beloît explained, pulling a half-burned stick from the fire pit and drawing an X on a fat birch tree. "Place your bets in my hat here." Pierre looked down at Beloît's greasy red cap. He remembered last summer when Beloît couldn't find a plate and ate his supper right out of that cap. It looked as if it hadn't been washed since then.

La Petite and Pierre each tossed in a coin. "We'll start at seven paces," Beloît said, counting his steps as he walked away from the stump. He scratched a line in the forest duff with the heel of his moccasin. The damp odor of the soil beneath the pine needles reminded Pierre of how his mother's flower garden smelled in early spring. Though Father teased her about "wasting good garden space on things a man can't eat," Pierre knew he was proud when the neighbors praised their colorful front yard.

Each man took a turn with his knife. Some were experienced throwers who balanced the bright steel lightly in their fingers and tossed with a quick swing of their arm. Others were amateurs who hit the tree with the flat side of their blades as often as they buried the point. One man even missed the tree altogether. And when Louie's knife hit handle first in the moss at the base of the tree, Beloît hollered, "Gads, Squeaks. Didn't your mama ever teach you back from front?"

Louie hung his head. "You'll hit it next time," Pierre said, clapping him on the shoulder.

But the most frightening toss of all was made by a drunken man named Balanger. When he drew back to throw, his knife slipped out of his hand and spun straight into the air. Everyone dove for the bushes. After the knife clattered off the hull of a canoe, Beloît leaped up and took a coin from his cap. Here's your money," he said. "You take a seat now and let the rest of us have a try."

When Pierre took his turn, the men whistled as he drew out his finely honed blade. "There's a real knife for you," La Petite said.

As the hand-tempered steel shined, Pierre thought of Charles La Londe, who had given him the knife just before the accident in which he had drowned.

Pierre's throw was low, but his blade pierced deep into the white bark, and the men gave a little cheer. Pierre was not very experienced at knife throwing. Though his mother had allowed him to whittle with his jackknife back home, she took it away whenever she caught him and his friends playing mumblety-peg or tossing their knives at a tree or fence post.

The man who most impressed Pierre with his knife throwing was the old sailor, Augustine. His first throw hit only an inch below the X. The more Pierre got to know Augustine, the more curious he became about the old sailor. He had powerful hands and arms that gave him a rugged, dangerous look, and he took great pride in his appearance. Unlike most of the men, who bathed only on Sunday afternoons, Augustine washed in the lake each evening, and he carefully shaved his bald head and face with his hunting knife. He kept his blade so sharp and handled his knife so deftly that no one but Beloît ever dared tease him.

Sensing that Augustine might win in the next round, Beloît said, "Not bad for an old sea dog, Auggie."

"My name is Augustine." He clenched his fist tight. As the muscles in his forearm flexed, the blue outline of a tattooed palm tree swayed back and forth.

"All right, Auggie," Beloît said.

Pierre couldn't believe Beloît's nerve. Augustine's eyes narrowed in rage, and he took a step toward Beloît. But just before he got within swinging distance, Beloît laughed, "Just kidding, old mate." Then he slapped Augustine's shoulder.

"It ain't mate," Augustine said stiffly, "and it ain't Auggie. And don't you ever forget it."

"All right, sailor, whatever you say," Beloît smiled, turning to the rest of the men. "Let's get on with it, boys."

Beloît's tactic worked; Augustine was so angry that he nearly missed the tree on his next try.

"Too bad, old salt," Beloît crowed. "Maybe you'll have an easier time at eight paces." Beloît measured the distance with his eye and drew his knife back. He missed the mark, and so did almost everyone else.

When Augustine's turn came, he stepped up and threw before Beloît had a chance to needle him. His blade flashed through the air and hit the X with a solid thunk. Everyone clapped the old sailor on the back. "Well thrown, monsieur," La Petite said.

"We'll see about that," Beloît mumbled, walking forward to examine the target. He pulled Augustine's blade out and tossed it to the ground. "You never touched the mark."

"What kind of bilge water is that?" Augustine shouted, trotting toward the birch.

"Look for yourself! We'll just have to divide these bets." Beloît reached for his coin-filled cap.

"Hands off!" Augustine hollered. He picked up his knife and turned toward Beloît.

"No!" Pierre shouted as Augustine's blade flashed through the air.

The knife grazed the back of Beloît's wrist and pinned his cap to the log. Beloît lifted his hand and stared at the bright channel of blood.

With a grin, Beloît reached down and pulled the knife from the log. As he stepped toward Augustine, he picked up his cap with his left hand. It was so quiet that Pierre could hear the rustling of a bird at the edge of the woods.

When Beloît reached Augustine, he pointed the knife

directly into his stomach, saying, "Now that's what I call a fine throw, Auggie." Then he flipped the knife toward him and handed him the capful of coins. "Here's your winnings."

Augustine caught his knife by the handle and re-sheathed it. He poured the coins into his hand and gave the cap back. "I earned the francs, but I don't want your filthy cap," he said, grinning slightly.

Beloît grinned then, too, and poking his finger through the knife hole, said, "A little extra ventilation won't hurt this old bonnet." He put his greasy cap back on his head, and the whole camp had a good laugh.

While Bellegarde started a campfire, Augustine pulled out a little sailor's pipe and played a lively jig. "Dance time," Beloît called. He wiped his bleeding wrist on his shirt front and began a wild dance. Others joined him, and soon the spirited group circled the campfire in a dizzying reel.

As the crazy bowman jigged, Pierre could see the light of the setting sun shining through the slit in Beloît's cap. Pierre was glad the men had declared a truce. How sad and stupid it would be to bury a man because of a senseless quarrel. Pierre hoped he would never again have to leave a broken paddle blade to mark a grave on a lonely shore like he had for La Londe.

# Chapter Five

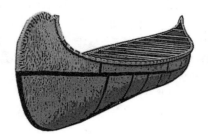

# Saganaga

"Time to voyage, *mesdemoiselles*!" Beloît yelled as he beat on Bellegarde's kettle with a spoon.

Pierre woke out of a sound sleep. Throwing off his blanket, he sat up and bumped his head on the ash thwart of the canoe.

It was 4 a.m., the usual time for departure, but after their long night of celebrating, the men were still snoring.

When Beloît saw that the kettle had little effect, he got out his Northwest gun. He winked at Pierre. "Tillie will wake these laggards from their dreams," he said, pouring a measure of powder down the barrel and ramming a patch home. He didn't bother to waste a ball.

Pierre closed his sleep-swollen eyes and covered his ears as Beloît drew back the hammer of his gun and pointed it skyward. Pierre shook his head, hoping Beloît would stop, but Beloit only gave a mean, ugly grin.

The whole world exploded when Beloît touched the trigger. Men leaped up and ran for their rifles. Bellegarde yelled, "Indians!" Louie tripped and fell into the ashes of the fire.

When the men realized what had happened, sticks, stones, and curses flew at Beloît. He just laughed.

After they boarded their canoes and started up North Lake, McHenry tried to soothe their raw nerves. "It's all downstream from here, gentlemen," he announced. Pierre looked into the still water. The commander must be joking. Though the map might say they'd reached the point where the waters flowed north, there wasn't any noticeable current yet.

Beloît was his usual cackling self, while the rest of the crew sat silent and glum, with yellowish complexions and black circles under their eyes.

But Pierre was amazed at how quickly the men recovered. By the midmorning breakfast stop, Beloît and Augustine were joking. "That sure was a fine party last night, eh?" Augustine said, as he wolfed down huge mouthfuls of the corn soup. "I ain't had such a fine time since the winter of '82 when I had a fortnight's shore leave in Bombay."

"Yes, indeed," Beloît agreed. "We only get to initiate *hommes du nord* once a year, and we got to do it proper." He grinned at Pierre. "Right, La Page?"

Pierre nodded.

Beloît walked over to Louie, who was lying face down on the ground. "Though it looks like we might have us a dead north man here." He paused to pack his pipe. "What do you think?" He nudged Louie's ribs with the toe of his moccasin. "Is it alive?"

Augustine laughed, "Looks like he's been flogged with a cat-o'-nine-tails and keelhauled."

While the men smoked, Pierre urged Louie to eat. "You've got to take a little food." Pierre remembered how weak he'd been during his first summer with a brigade. "You'll never make it through the day if you don't." He finally convinced Louie to drink some water and take a few spoonfuls of lukewarm corn.

"What's McHenry got his sights on?" La Petite rose from his seat at the base of a white pine. The commander was standing by the canoes, staring at the horizon. Pierre followed La Petite to the shore.

"Fire?" La Petite asked McHenry.

McHenry nodded. "By that smoke plume I'd say it's a right big blaze."

Pierre saw a thin yellow wisp above the horizon.

"Should I get your glass?" La Petite asked. The commander carried a small brass telescope in a varnished box.

"No need," McHenry said. "We'll just have to keep our eyes on the wind. It hasn't rained in some places since May. Back at the fort they said that fires have been burning on and off all summer.

"Any big ones?" La Petite asked.

I heard that a hundred square miles have burned up already."

La Petite whistled softly as the three of them studied the distant smoke trail.

Later that morning, Pierre's brigade met an XY Fur Company crew at Wooden Horse Falls portage. The XY traders had just unloaded their canoes and were getting ready to portage.

Though Commander McHenry hailed the group with a civil, "Morning, gentlemen," he received only sneers in return.

Beloît jumped in. "Are you Potties lost here in the big wood?" Potties was an insulting nickname for the English traders. "You're a long way from your mamas' laps."

Curses flew between the groups.

In the middle of the ruckus Beloît shouted, *"Je suis l'homme."*

That brought a broad-shouldered XY man forward. "Any pig can squeal," he said. "How about backing up that mouth with a little contest?"

"Name it," Beloît snapped.

"Would a race from here to Saganaga Lake be too much for you?"

"Done."

The Nor'Westers scrambled to unload. A pair of men shouldered each canoe, while the rest, double-packed, headed up the trail. Pierre would have enjoyed pausing to view the rapids if he'd had time. A white funnel of foam roared through a bare chasm of rock, then plunged over a three-stage drop where the water fell thirty feet into a roiling pool.

It took several trips to haul all the goods across the portage, and the brigades taunted each other the whole time. Pierre knew that men were supposed to yield to anyone carrying a canoe, but when Beloît and Bellegarde tried to portage their canoe, an XY man blocked their way. Beloît yelled, "Get out of my way, Pottie boy."

The XY man tossed down his packs and turned to fight, but McHenry intervened. "I'll dock a month's pay from any man who raises his fists," he said. Beloît spat and continued on his way.

Since the XY brigade had a head start, they began their last carry ahead of the Nor'Westers. La Petite led the final group up the trail, followed closely by Pierre and Louie. Though La Petite was carrying three packs, the boys still had to jog to keep up with his giant strides.

On the top of the last ridge La Petite suddenly stopped. Pierre plowed into him, and Louie, who was following close behind, tripped over Pierre's feet and crashed to the ground.

La Petite shouted a curse.

For a moment Pierre thought La Petite was yelling at him and Louie. Then he saw the boulder. The last group of XY men had rolled a huge rock into the trail and piled several windfall logs across the path.

"Those low-down, scum-sucking dogs," the big man

growled. "In all my living days, I never ..." Still cursing, he threw down his packs and began clearing the trail. Even with Pierre and Louie's help, there was soon a backup of angry voyageurs.

When they finally reached the end of the portage, anger turned to outrage. Someone had caved in the bow of one of their canoes with a cannonball-size rock. Though the XY brigade was out of sight and Wooden Horse Falls was roaring in the background, Beloît bellowed a curse down the lake.

"Save your strength," McHenry said, studying the damaged canoe. It was clearly beyond repair. "La Petite?"

"Aye, Sir."

"We'll take your canoe and make an express run to Saganaga. Those Ojibwe on the north shore still make canoes, don't they?"

"Near as I know."

"It will cost us dearly, no doubt, but we have no choice," McHenry said, studying the damaged canoe. "We'll need two parcels of trade goods and a keg of rum. Let's take two—no, make it four—extra paddlers to bring the new boat back."

Pierre was glad when La Petite signaled for him to come along. He was impressed by the commander's decisiveness. Though McHenry normally let his foreman manage things, he was clearly in charge now. When the small crew was ready to leave, he turned to those staying behind with one last order. "You fellows see that the freight is ready to load as soon as we get back."

Pierre was amazed at the speed of the north canoe without freight. It rode a foot higher in the water, and with two extra paddlers in the bow and stern, it skimmed down the Granite River like a ship under sail.

Tight lipped, the voyageurs paddled without their usual jokes and songs. To Pierre, the silence made the river cold and lonely. Usually McHenry consulted his charts and journals while they were underway, but now he took up a paddle and helped.

The men crossed one short portage at a trot and *saulted*, or shot, two rapids that they never would have tried in a loaded canoe. "Pull hard," Beloît hollered at the head of the Mariboo Rapids, allowing La Petite time to turn the boat straight down stream. Time stopped as their blades whirled above the whitewater and the canoe shot through the waves. It was easy for Pierre to see how the Granite River got its name. On both sides sheer granite walls rose up, unbroken except for a few mossy ledges that harbored pale clumps of lichens and stunted pines.

As McHenry predicted, the Ojibwe band on Saganaga bartered hard, demanding a full keg of rum and an assortment of goods for a north canoe. Though McHenry tried to talk them into accepting just trade goods, the Indians were set on rum.

"I hate the liquor trade," he said. Pierre's commander had said the same thing the previous year. "The more of them the rum kills, the more they want it. The cycle has got us all trapped."

It was late afternoon by the time they made it back to Wooden Horse Falls. Pierre assumed that the brigade would camp for the night, but the men had other plans.

The voyageurs paddled with the energy of men possessed. They remained silent and kept their eyes fixed downstream. No one hummed or even whistled.

It was after sunset when the crew reached Saganaga Lake. Pierre's arms ached, and his right hand was a cramped claw from clutching his paddle. His soreness reminded him of the blisters that had plagued him the summer before. He was glad they would soon stop for the night.

But the brigade struck straight across the lake. "How long is Saganaga?" Pierre turned and asked La Petite.

"Ten miles or so," La Petite said, unfazed by the

gathering darkness. "The grand thing about this lake is the islands. A friend of mine counted two hundred before he gave up."

"It looks like we're going to see exactly zero on this trip," Pierre replied.

The men kept their same steady pace under the black sky. Last summer Pierre had learned to "trick" away his work by dreaming about other things, but in the dark it was hard to think of anything but his sore hands. Would they ever stop?

"I hope you know how to steer by the stars," Pierre said, searching the black sky.

"As long as I can see the North Star and the Dipper, I can navigate all the way to Hudson's Bay." La Petite spoke in a low voice, as if he were afraid to disturb the stillness.

An hour later the brigade rounded a point, and Beloît suddenly stopped paddling. He called back in a hoarse whisper, "There they are."

Everyone held his paddle still. Pierre stared down the bay. At the far end of the lake—perhaps a mile distant—a campfire flickered.

"Now we got 'em," La Petite growled. Pierre shivered. So the men intended to get back at the XY Company! But what would they do? Murder the fellows in their sleep?

McHenry's canoe drifted alongside La Petite's. "Shall we take that campsite in the south bay?" La Petite asked.

"You're not planning a nighttime visit to our XY friends, are you?" By McHenry's voice, Pierre could tell he was smiling.

"It is a fine evening to go calling, sir."

"Tell me no more," McHenry replied, shifting to his commander's voice. "But I must warn you that McTavish wants no more bloodshed."

"Aye, sir," La Petite answered. "But first we'll have a little supper."

After they paddled back around the point and out of

sight, Bellegarde cooked the men a quick meal. They ate fast and dispensed with their usual bragging and story telling. Later, as they sat pulling on their clay pipes under the starlit sky, La Petite suddenly said, "Listen."

At first Pierre could hear nothing. Then he caught the distant sound of singing. Beloît's devilish face, lit by the embers of the fire, broke into a grin. "Just as I hoped. They're celebrating."

La Petite nodded. "They'll be sleeping heavy tonight." He turned to Pierre. "You want to help us pay those Potties a visit?"

As tired as he was, Pierre was curious. "Why not?" He nodded, but even as he agreed, he wondered if it was wise to go along.

McHenry rose and said, "Good night." He bent down to light a candle in the coals of the fire, then walked toward his tent. Just before he closed the flap, he said, "Take care of yourselves, lads."

Pierre studied the distorted shadows that danced across the tent wall as McHenry set his candle down, reached into his book crate, and settled back for his nightly ritual.

"Reading," Beloît snorted. "If that ain't a waste of good candles."

Two hours later a single canoe headed up the lake toward the XY camp. The fire they'd noticed earlier had burned down to a dim orange dot. They carried a half dozen rifles. "Pack one for each man, just in case," La Petite had said. Beloît had stowed a single pack sack in the bow.

As they neared the camp, Pierre tried to stay calm. What if the XY men awoke? Beloît would have no qualms about using his gun. Two traders had been murdered by XY men last spring. Imagine his mother's face when she found out he'd been shot during a midnight raid on a rival camp!

From fifty yards off shore Pierre could hear snoring.

"This is going to be too easy," Beloît whispered loudly. La Petite shushed him.

Using hand signals, the men paddled around to the back side of the island and stepped silently ashore. Beloît opened his pack and whispered, "This little gimlet should do the trick." He pulled out a little tee-handled drill. Next he drew out a pistol and shoved it into the red sash at his waist.

La Petite shook his head and said, "No, Jean," but Beloît only patted the handle and said, "Just in case …"

Still shaking his head, La Petite followed him into the darkness with Pierre close behind.

Their moccasins were quiet as they crept over the mossy ground toward the camp. When they got within sight of the campfire, they dropped to their knees. The heavy breathing of the XY men hinted that they'd partied as hard as Beloît had hoped.

When Beloît saw the rum kegs, he grinned so widely that Pierre could see his dirty teeth shining in the starlight. Though a man was sleeping under a canoe only two yards away, Beloît was calm. Handing a keg to La Petite and Pierre, he motioned for them to pass it on. One by one the men relayed the kegs back into the shadows. Pierre's heart raced each time an XY man rolled over in his sleep or sighed. If someone shouted an alarm, the odds would be four to one against them.

In a few minutes they'd carried ten kegs into the quiet of the woods. There Beloît knelt with a soft chuckle. "We'll take one for ourselves, and I'll fix the rest good," he said. Grinning, he bored a hole in each keg with his gimlet. As the liquor trickled out onto the ground, Beloît chuckled, and La Petite had to cuff his head to quiet him.

When the job was finally done, the men started back to their canoe. But Beloît said, "Wait."

Everyone stopped, and La Petite waved his hand and said, "Let's go."

Beloit shook his head. "We've got to stack them back up."

"What?" La Petite whispered.

"Can't you see what a great joke it will be?" Beloît insisted. "They'll get up in the morning, thinking everything is normal, but when they go to load their kegs ..."

"All right, all right," La Petite whispered to quiet him.

Pierre's heart was pounding harder than ever as they relayed the kegs back into place. The XY men were sleeping more fitfully now, and it was only a matter of time before someone woke up.

Beloît was setting the last keg in place when an XY man sat up and mumbled, "What's that?" Before the fellow could say another word, Beloît pulled out his pistol and clubbed him on the side of the head. Then, catching the unconscious man by the shoulders, he laid him quietly back on his blanket.

The entire crew froze. Pierre waited for someone else to sit up or shout. Across the fire a man coughed and rolled over. Pierre was sure that someone would hear his heart pounding, but the ragged snoring continued.

It's got to be the rum, Pierre thought as his crew began crawling back toward the shelter of the woods. When Pierre reached the shadows, he heard a dull, scratching sound. He turned, amazed to see Beloît drilling a hole in the bottom an XY canoe. Pierre looked at La Petite, who shrugged and motioned for the men to move on.

As soon as their canoe was in the water, La Petite handed each man a rifle. A battle looked inevitable. A few minutes later, there was a rustling in the underbrush. Pierre heard a rifle cock to his left, and he lifted his own gun to his shoulder.

Pierre saw a shadowy figure at the edge of the woods. A second rifle cocked in the dark. Pierre was feeling for his trigger when a voice croaked, "*Je suis l'homme.*" Then he saw Beloît's ugly grin.

As the men lowered their rifles, La Petite mumbled, "Can you believe that?" Beloît was waving the XY commander's plumed top hat above his head.

When Beloît reached the men, he declared, "I got no use for fancy hats, but these are some real fine feathers." He set the elegant hat on the ground and placed his fat moccasin on the crown. Crushing it flat, he pulled the elegant ostrich plumes from the band and sailed the hat out over the dark lake. Long after the splash, Beloît was still enjoying a wicked chuckle.

# Chapter Six

# Night Journey

As they paddled up the lake, the still water sparkled with starlight, and a thin slip of moon hung above the black shore. The quiet reminded Pierre of a night last spring when he and his father had speared northern pike in a stream near their house. In an hour they'd filled a washtub with fish and were ready to start home. "No sense wasting lamp oil," Father had said.

When Father turned the wick down, the world went black. Then as Pierre's eyes adjusted, the moonlight gradually illuminated the woods and the dew-flecked fields beyond.

Now, with the excitement over, Pierre felt the effects of his all-day paddle. He was looking forward to a sound sleep. But when they returned to the North West camp, the canoes were all loaded.

"What's going on?" Pierre asked La Petite. Was the moonlight tricking his eyes?

"We can't stop now," he said. "We've got to put some miles between us and those Potties before they wake up."

"What?" Pierre said. He couldn't believe his ears.

"We've got to get clear of Saganaga tonight."

Augustine nodded. "He's right, mate. If we tried to paddle past that island after daybreak, we'd be eating musket balls for breakfast."

The brigade struck out across the lake and paddled in silence past the XY camp. They never stopped until they portaged into Cypress Lake in the early morning hours. Pierre was astonished at the endurance of the men. The day dawned hot and sunny, and smoke from the big fire that was smoldering south of Saganaga Lake sometimes drifted over the canoes and burned Pierre's eyes. But the old timers were too busy joking about the XY brigade to care about the heat or the smoke. They'd slept less than four hours in the last day and a half, yet they pulled steadily on their paddles.

"We sure got them Potties, eh, Auggie?" Beloît called to Augustine.

The old sailor grinned, accepting the nickname. "We gave 'em exactly what they deserved."

Beloît threw back his head and laughed, snorting through his deformed nose.

Louie was having a hard time. The aftereffects of the rum, along with the lack of sleep, had left him so sick he could barely sit up to paddle. When Pierre asked him how he was doing, he said, "Death would be an improvement."

Though Louie could only manage a single pack on the portages, no one teased him except Beloît. The more the crewmen pitied Louie, the more Beloît picked on him. After crossing Swamp Portage just after dawn, Louie had sat on a rock to catch his breath. Beloît called to him. "You sure are quiet today, Noise Box. I appreciate it so much that I got you a present." The bowman was crouched in knee-high grass and grinning as if he'd found a treasure. When Louie walked over, Beloît picked up a half-rotted muskrat carcass by the tail and dangled it in front of his face.

Louie turned green and gagged, while Beloît feigned surprise. Beloit kept up the same tricks all day. On another portage he snuck up behind Louie and goosed him with a wet canoe paddle. During a pipe stop on Little Knife Lake he "accidentally" blew pipe smoke into Louie's face.

"Why don't you leave him be?" Pierre said. He sat down beside Louie and offered him a drink from his tin cup.

"Look," Beloît said, tapping his clay pipe on the side of a tree and letting the ashes fall on Pierre's moccasins. "Squeaks has found himself a little nurse maid."

Beloît didn't care if no one else laughed. Though most of the men got quieter as the day went on, Beloît got louder. And the more Pierre tried to protect Louie, the meaner Beloît got. Pierre thought about giving up, but when he remembered how La Londe had helped him last summer, he vowed to do the same for Louie.

By midday, Pierre had paddled beyond tiredness. His palms felt like he was holding hot coals. His arms were stiff and aching. The closest he'd ever come to being this exhausted had happened last fall. One Saturday morning he and his father were bucking up firewood with a two-man crosscut saw—a "misery whip" his father called it—and Pierre was anxious to prove that his first summer as a voyageur had made him into a man.

"You ready for a break?" Father had asked, after they'd been sawing steadily for an hour.

"I'm fine," Pierre had replied. So they went on pulling the big saw back and forth, cutting up block after block of wood.

When Father asked, "You tired yet?" Pierre shook his head. Though his hair was plastered to his forehead with sweat and his hands were raw, he had to show Father he could match any pace that he set.

Pierre could see a steely determination in Father's eyes, and he knew there would be no more offers of rest. It would be up to Pierre to call the contest off. The blade ripped back and forth. The sugary scent of maple burned in Pierre's nostrils as the sawdust piled over the toes of his boots. They lifted a new log into place. The blade started again.

Mother saved them both by calling them to lunch. As sore as Pierre's body was that afternoon, it ached twice as much the next day.

Now Pierre wondered how he would feel after two days and a night of brutal paddling.

It was noon when they stopped for a smoke at Thunder Point on Knife Lake. "Do you suppose we're clear of those XY upstarts by now, Commander?" La Petite asked McHenry.

McHenry turned to Beloît before he answered. "How many holes did you bore in that canoe, Jean?"

"A half dozen, sir" Beloît replied.

McHenry smiled. "No doubt they'll have to bargain for a new canoe same as we did. I'd say it's plenty safe to camp here."

"Aye, sir," La Petite replied. "We'll not see those Potties this side of the border."

"Agreed then."

Those words were heaven sent for Pierre. After thirty-some hours without sleep he felt as if he were floating high above the water, looking down on himself. Every sound, from the voices to the calls of the shorebirds and the lapping of the waves against the hull, was miles away.

"Wake up, La Page," Beloît yelled. "You gonna help us make camp? Or you gonna play sick like your little lady friend here?" Startled, Pierre looked up. Beloît had stepped into the shallow water and was jabbing Louie in the ribs with a paddle. Louie's head was slumped over a pack sack, and all he could do was moan.

Augustine wet a kerchief and sponged off Louie's sunburned neck.

"Ow," Louie groaned, opening his eyes.

"I know it hurts," the old sailor said, "but a little cool

water will take away the sting. I've gotten scorched a few times myself. The worst was off the coast of Morocco when I was about your age. You've had too much grog and too much sun—that's like being hit with a hurricane at high tide."

Even though Beloît called him "Little Lou's Mama," Augustine helped the boy out of the canoe.

When Pierre stood up to get out of the canoe, he was so stiff that he almost fell backward.

In fifteen minutes the canoes were unloaded and the campfire was lit. Pierre stood on the shore for a moment and admired Knife Lake. Their campsite was on a point that jutted out from the south shore. Towering white pines offered a canopy that filtered the light to a soft, mottled green. A deep carpet of pine needles, dry from weeks without rain, crunched beneath Pierre's moccasins. A gentle breeze from the west kept the mosquitoes away.

While Bellegarde's soup pot boiled, the men inspected the hulls of their canoes and shared stories of the raid on the XY camp. They regummed the seams with balsam pitch. The bow of Pierre's canoe needed a short length of *wattape*, the spruce root lacing that held the birchbark sheets together.

Long after dinner was done, the members of the brigade were still laughing and bragging about how they'd showed up those Potties. Beloît was the hero of everyone's story. "Why after we was done with the rum kegs and ready to turn tail," Augustine said, "Jean Beloît took out his gimlet and riddled one of their boats with holes. And to top it all off he stole the hat of the..."

Pierre smiled. He knew the story would get a little better each time it was told. By next spring Beloît would be known as the man who'd single-handedly humiliated an entire XY brigade.

As the fire was dying down to coals, Augustine offered to pipe a tune if anyone cared to dance. To Pierre's amazement, a dozen men volunteered.

With a tired grin, McHenry retired to his tent. For once the commander lit no candle. "It looks like our leader is too tired to read tonight," Pierre said to La Petite.

"He may not feel like reading, but he could go another two days without rest if he needed to." When Pierre frowned in disbelief, La Petite continued. "McHenry may not look the part, but there's not a tougher man this side of Lake Athabasca."

"All he does is sit in his tent and read," Pierre said. Pierre loved literature too, but when saw a pale, bookish fellow like McHenry, he hated to admit it. "He looks like he's spent his whole life locked up in a library."

"Don't let that pasty complexion fool you," La Petite said. "He might be a reader, but he's a doer, too. When the time comes, you'll see what I mean."

Pierre didn't believe a word of it. If going to college meant he would grow up to be a frail bookworm like McHenry, he wanted no part of it. Forget his mother's dreams of his becoming a doctor or a lawyer. He would spend the rest of his life as a canoeman.

# Chapter Seven

# Wild Fire

Pierre awoke to the sound of hooves clattering on rock. The Potties are attacking, he thought. But where would they get horses? As his mind shook off the sleep fog, he tossed his blanket aside and rolled out from under the canoe. The moon was down and the pines were swaying in a strong wind that had switched to the southeast.

Puffs of yellow smoke swirled in the predawn light. Pierre looked toward the shore. For a moment, he thought he saw a caribou running past McHenry's tent. He rubbed his eyes. There were two more animals charging out of the woods and leaping into the water. More of the herd followed. All of the men were on their feet now. Beloît was leveling his gun on the nearest caribou when McHenry suddenly shouted, "No, Jean."

The "Jean" sounded strange, since the men rarely called Beloît by his first name, but it got his attention.

"What the ... " Beloît protested. "That's a week's worth of meat."

"Listen," McHenry shouted, grabbing Beloît's gun barrel in his hand. The whole camp was quieted by the urgency in McHenry's voice.

Pierre heard a distant crackle over the gusts of wind.

"It's a forest fire!" McHenry hollered. "Load up, men. We've got to get clear of this shore."

Pierre had never been close to a wildfire, but he'd heard stories about updrafts that generated terrific winds. The Saganaga Lake fire had turned with the wind and was rushing straight for them.

The men loaded their canoes in seconds, heaping the packs, parcels, and kegs in each boat and grabbing their paddles. By the time the crew scrambled into their canoes, the roar of the fire was so loud that McHenry's hollered, "Double time," sounded like a choked whisper.

Along with the swirling clouds of smoke, hot cinders blew out of the pines and hit the men on their backs and arms. The hot ashes were particularly painful, since most of the men had been sleeping naked in the heat. Beloît, who was standing in the bow, slapped several hot pine needles off his shoulders without comment, but when a flaming ember landed on his buttocks, he let out a yelp that made everyone laugh.

Their laughter came to a sudden stop, when just down the shore, a squirrel leaped from the crown of a burning pine with a demon-like shriek, its back and tail blazing. Pierre watched in horror as the poor creature hit the lake with a sickening hiss of steam. Next a fox and then a marten scampered out of the woods, their eyes white with fear as they dove into the water.

A moment later rippling flames engulfed the campsite they had occupied only minutes earlier. The men stared open-mouthed as an orange tongue of flame, driven by a gust of wind, shot out over the water and rolled up into the sky. Thick, black smoke swirled across the lake, and the surface was coated with ash.

Pierre stared at the inferno. Though the water stopped the fire from reaching their canoes, further down the bay the flames jumped across a narrow arm of the lake.

"Blessed Mother of God," Pierre heard Louie whisper

behind him. He turned and saw the same look of fear and wonder on every face.

"You suppose it's too early for breakfast?" Beloît's voice drowned out the fading din of the fire. "If we're gonna sit and gawk at this old fire, we might as well put on the soup pot." When they looked at him standing naked in the bow, everyone had to laugh. Leave it to Beloît to think of his stomach at a time like this.

# Chapter Eight

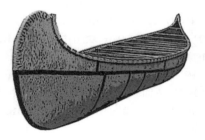

# Pictographs

The voyageurs stopped at the west end of Knife Lake to repack their hastily loaded goods. The dirty pink of the sunrise revealed a blackened landscape to the south. A burned smell lingered in the air. Pierre stared at the devastation. Though most of the trees had been incinerated by the fire, a scattering of green crowns showed that the flames had skipped over some pockets of pines. Pierre was glad that a few of the majestic trees had been spared.

After breakfast the brigade started over the Knife Lake Portage. Pierre had just started up the trail when he stepped on a shiny, black rock and yelled, "Ouch."

As Pierre hopped up and down, Augustine called, "Should I pipe a little tune for you?"

"Big Knife Portage can be mighty rough on moccasins," La Petite said. "The Indians used to quarry some of the rocks on Knife Lake for tools and weapons."

Once they finished the carry, the brigade made excellent time. They crossed Carp and Birch Lakes with favorable winds, and portaged the Great Whitewood

Carrying Place, a sweeping curve above a split stream that fell in a series of rushing cascades into Basswood Lake.

As they boarded their canoes and started up Basswood, McHenry took a turn in La Petite's canoe. During the trip he switched from one canoe to another, giving each crew a turn at sharing the burden of an extra passenger. Since the wind was now out of the northwest—the very course they were on—Pierre was not excited about taking extra weight in his canoe. A crate of the commander's books came with him, too.

McHenry sat just ahead of Pierre and Louie. Before they'd taken a dozen paddle strokes, La Petite said, "You know, Commander, young La Page here is quite a scholar."

"Is that so?" McHenry turned and smiled at Pierre.

Pierre blushed as Beloît chortled, "That's right, sir. If he could paddle as well as he can do his school work, we'd be at Rainy River by now." The men laughed.

McHenry ignored Beloît. "Did you go to the Catholic school in Lachine?"

Pierre nodded. He hated being the center of attention. Beloît would tease him forever if he started talking about school!

"Those sisters are a dedicated lot," McHenry said. "You're fortunate to have teachers who love learning. I'll bet you read lots of poetry."

"Yes, sir, we did." Pierre smiled as he thought back to his teacher, Sister Anne. She urged him to study things deeply and to never be satisfied with simple answers. "We are born to inquire after the truth," she would often say, quoting Montaigne. She also quoted the Greek philosopher Plato: "The life which is unexamined is not worth living."

The canoes turned into the main part of the lake, and the full force of the wind hit them. Green whitecaps rolled out of the northwest, threatening to swamp any canoe that veered from an upwind course. The men feathered their paddles, turning the edge of the blades into the wind on their forward reach and then pulling back hard through the roiling foam.

"Did you read much Latin poetry?" McHenry ignored the terrific wind.

Pierre nodded, wishing the commander would drop the subject.

But McHenry continued. "How about Horace and Ovid?"

"Sister Anne loved them both. Last spring we had to memorize a long section of Metamorphoses and ..."

That was too much for Beloît. "Talk French, you two," he hollered from the bow. "How can a man navigate a canoe with all this silly blabbering about poets?" He spit out the p in poets as if it were a cuss word.

McHenry chuckled, doffing his tall hat before it could blow off in the wind. "Our gentle bowman is right," he said, "and considering the weather, it might be wise of me to lend a hand."

The commander slipped off his coat and took up a paddle. Pierre was surprised at how quickly he picked up the rhythm. As Beloît sang, "Pull, pull, pull," from the bow, the commander's muscles rippled beneath his loose, white shirt. Though McHenry looked thin and frail, Pierre could sense a whipcord strength in his arms and shoulders.

Paddling hard across the Z-shaped lake, they passed a Hudson's Bay Post on the north side and an Indian village that lay on a long point to the south. There was little talk as the men focused on the waves, holding their blades when the bow rose high on a foaming crest, and pulling when the canoe dipped into a green trough. Everyone but Beloît looked tense. When the wind was at its worst and Pierre was measuring the distance to a nearby island for a possible swim in case they swamped, Beloît laughed and hollered, "Hold on to your hats, *hivernants*."

At last they reached the lee shore of Basswood Lake. Though the crowns of the tall white pines were swaying and creaking in the wind, the rock ledge where they camped was sheltered. While the men unloaded the canoes, McHenry excused himself. "I'd help you, lads," the commander explained, handing his paddle to Pierre, "but these mitts can't stand much abuse these days."

Taking the paddle from McHenry, Pierre saw what he meant. The tips of his fingers were a lumpy mass of scar tissue, and his fingernails were cracked and bleeding. At that moment Pierre realized that McHenry usually kept his fingers curled to conceal these scars. This was the first time that Pierre had gotten a close look at his hands.

As soon as the commander was out of ear shot, Pierre turned to La Petite. "Where did he get those terrible marks on his hands?"

"I told you the commander's been through a lot," La Petite handed a pack to Pierre. "You should ask him about it sometime."

Pierre tried to think what could have caused such terrible wounds. An animal bite? An accident with a machine?

Supper was a quiet affair for a change, and as soon as Pierre finished eating, he crawled under the nearest canoe and collapsed onto his blanket. His legs were sore, and his back and arms ached as badly as they had the previous summer. Despite his tiredness, Pierre slept fitfully.

A tangled dream woke him once during the night. He was standing beside Celeste on the pier back in Lachine where ships docked to pick up furs and deliver goods to the North West depot. Though it was midday, the waterfront was oddly quiet. A strange canoe floated by. It was painted black and covered with an arched, birchbark top like an Ojibwe grave house. As the bow of the canoe turned in the current, Pierre saw Kennewah's body lying still and cold. Her hands were folded across her chest, and her eyes were staring straight up.

"No," Pierre whispered, but when Celeste turned to see what was wrong, the body had changed. It was Jean Beloît, pale and white and dead.

Pierre woke with a start. The wind was still howling through the pines overhead, and for a moment he couldn't remember where he was. It took him a long time to calm the beating of his heart. He rubbed his eyes. As he thought about the hazy line that divided dreams from reality, he recalled a quote painted on the wall above Sister Anne's blackboard: "We are such stuff as dreams are made on, and our little life is rounded with a sleep."

Pierre breathed in the scent of cold ashes and pine needles. He tried to clear the picture of Kennewah from his mind, but for the remainder of the night, there was no escaping the cold vacancy of her eyes.

Calm weather settled in for the next few days, and the brigade took advantage of the perfect conditions. By rising early and paddling hard, they made near-record time.

Before breakfast the men took the Little Basswood, Great Pine, and Little Stone portages. In the dawn mist, the Basswood River was a thundering cataract, surging over rugged outcroppings of granite streaked with quartz. It was high summer, and the whole of the north was bursting with life. The rocky paths were bordered by green clumps of bunchberries, delicate ferns, and feathery ground pines. Warblers and thrushes bobbed through the undergrowth, while jays and nuthatches flitted through the branches overhead.

A mile into Crooked Lake the brigade paddled past a tall granite cliff that was streaked with many colors. As they drew closer, Pierre noticed shapes painted on the rock face. "Look, La Petite," he said, "a picture of a moose and a canoe filled with men."

"That it is," he replied as the men shipped their paddles and went into a silent glide. "It looks like a war canoe."

"And see there beside it," Louie said. "There's a sun, a human hand, and a crane."

Pierre admired the rich red tone of the artwork. Each picture was drawn at the height a man could reach while standing in a canoe, or perhaps on the ice?

"Where did they get the paint?" Louie asked.

"And what do the figures stand for?" Pierre asked.

"No one knows," La Petite answered. "They've been here as long as anyone Indian or white can remember."

"I've heard that they used iron oxide and fish oil for the paint," McHenry spoke from the trailing canoe. Pierre studied some of the weirder shapes. There was a man with horns curling up from his head, a sea monster, a strange disk shape, and a gnome-like face.

Pierre wondered what sort of people had lived on this lake years ago? Were these pictures of their gods? Their hopes? Their dreams?

"The one thing we know for sure," La Petite said, pointing upward, "is that those are Sioux arrows."

Pierre tilted his head back. At least two dozen arrows protruded from a tiny cleft near the top of the cliff.

"According to the story," La Petite said, "a Sioux war party came through this country and left those arrows to warn the Ojibwe that they might return at any time."

McHenry nodded. "It may have been the same bunch of Sioux that butchered La Vérendrye's party up on Massacre Island."

"Let's not waste the whole day jabbering," Beloît interrupted. "Paddle!"

"Aye, aye, sir," Augustine joked, and the crew all laughed as they took up their paddles again.

The brigade pushed steadily inland. The weather was so hot that the men paddled bare-chested, and Beloît wore only a breechclout and his dirty red cap.

The only incident to mar their day occurred at the Curtain Falls Portage. Pierre was walking just ahead of Beloît and Louie, who were carrying a North canoe. Louie slipped on some loose rocks and yelled. Though Beloît managed to keep the canoe from sliding over the ledge, Louie fell.

Beloît and Pierre ran to the edge of the trail. The black water below was still. Pierre could hear the rapids downstream. Last summer his friend La Londe had perished just as suddenly.

"There he is." Beloît pointed to a ledge about twenty feet below. Louie was lying on an outcropping above the river. He wasn't moving and his left arm was folded under his body, but Pierre prayed that he was alive. Pierre could already see the North West Company courier, hat in hand, delivering the news to Louie's mother that her son was never coming home.

Pierre, Maurice, and Beloît climbed down the cliff, careful not to dislodge any rocks. When they got to Louie, he was unconscious and there was a cut above his right eye, but he was breathing evenly. "That's a good sign," Beloît said, as they lifted him onto a blanket and carried him carefully back up to the trail.

They laid him in the shade of a big spruce, and as soon as McHenry dabbed some cold water on Louie's forehead, his eyes fluttered open. "What ..." Louie faltered. "What hit me?"

His confusion worried Pierre, but by the time the rest of the brigade had finished the portage, Louie was sitting up. He grinned weakly at Pierre and said, "I'll bet you thought you were going to have to make a grave marker out of my paddle."

"Lie down and rest," Pierre said.

When Louie obeyed, the commander took Pierre aside. "With a blow to the head like that, it's important that you don't let him fall asleep."

Pierre sat beside Louie until nightfall, telling his friend stories and reciting silly poems until McHenry finally said that it was safe to let him rest.

By the next morning, Louie was back to his old chattering self. "Noise Box," Beloît shouted, "if you don't pipe down, I'm gonna take you back to that cliff and pitch you off again."

# Chapter Nine

# Crane Lake Fort

Two days later McHenry's brigade reached the North West Company fort at Crane Lake. They were greeted by a volley of cheers, and as they neared the shore, a grizzled fellow discharged a rusty musket skyward. With a toothless grin the old man watched his load of birdshot rain down on the canoes.

"Now that's what I call a fine hello," Beloît said.

After talking a few minutes with old friends, the men unloaded their canoes. Pierre had just finished his second trip to the fort when he caught the black sheen of a girl's hair out of the corner of his eye.

"Kennewah," Pierre called. "Kenne ..." He stopped as a pretty Ojibwe girl turned toward him. She smiled.

Pierre lowered his eyes. It was so easy to forget that Kennewah and her whole family were gone.

"What you squealing at, La Page?" Beloît snarled.

"Nothing," Pierre replied, digging the toe of his moccasin into the sandy path.

"Well, let's finish unloading. It's your turn to haul them blasted books."

Pierre lifted McHenry's crate to his shoulder and hurried toward the front gate.

After a two-day stop at the fort, McHenry split his brigade into two groups. One crew headed north to Quetico Lake, while McHenry took Pierre's party south to Lake Vermilion. Pierre hoped McHenry would send Beloît north with the other group, but the commander kept the crew in each canoe intact. At least La Petite and Louie would be going with him.

The Vermilion River emptied into Crane Lake only a few hundred yards from the fort at a rapids called The Chute. Here the brigade made a predawn carry to start their thirty-mile river journey.

The Chute was a white funnel of foam that surged between two huge, rounded boulders. "Last month," La Petite said, raising his voice over the rushing water, "a fellow slipped as he was stepping out of his canoe up there. One of his mates grabbed for him, but it was too late. When they found the body, his face looked like he'd dived into a brick yard."

Pierre shuddered as he studied the powerful rapids. A single misstep was all it took. On the ridge above, Pierre saw a red painted paddle blade, broken in half and tied in the shape of a cross to honor the man's death.

At sunrise the brigade portaged past a spectacular stretch of water called The Gorge. Here the portage trail ran high above a deep chasm. Funneled between sheer rock walls, the water rushed over black boulders and ledges. In places the path was only half a step from the cliff's edge. Thinking back to Louie's near tragedy at Curtain Falls, Pierre watched his footing carefully.

Beloît teased him at a pose halfway through the carry. "Want to try a little cliff diving?" He elbowed Pierre towards the edge. "The trick is to not kiss any rocks." When Pierre's eyes got big, Beloît gave his usual hoarse laugh. "I'm only joshing, bookworm."

Upstream of the Gorge the current slowed. The river was low and marshy with wild rice beds lining both banks for long stretches. Once, as the canoes cut past a high point of land, an osprey dove down and grabbed a fish out of the water only ten feet in front of their bow. Beloît didn't see the bird until it hit the water, and he let out a high-pitched "Eeeek."

As the osprey flew up with the fish, water splashed into Beloît's face. The crew roared.

"Who's that little woman screeching in the bow?" La Petite called.

"Call her Millie," Augustine said. "She sure is an ugly one."

"Shut yer yaps," Beloît yelled. "I thought we was being attacked."

"Attacked?" Augustine laughed again. "Those birds can really be scary. Just think if it had been a giant woodpecker, Jean. He'd a gone right after your paddle."

"Or maybe his wooden head?" Pierre offered, and the whole crew roared.

"Paddle!" Beloît shouted. For once he was at a loss for words.

The scenery was spectacular along the Vermilion River, and other than Table Rock Falls, which required a mile-long carry, the portages were easy. Stately pines lined the ridges, and the quiet bays were dotted with yellow and white water lilies that gave off a heady scent. When they cut close to a rocky headland, Pierre caught the warm smell of blueberries.

McHenry said, "This country reminds me of the pastoral poetry of Lucretius. Do you know his work, La Page?"

"Spare us that sissy talk," Beloît crowed.

Pierre blushed. He'd studied Lucretius, but he shook his head.

"Thank the Lord for small favors," Beloît said.

At midday Beloît spotted a moose at the river's edge,

but it lumbered into the woods before he could get his gun up.

"Millie is not so quick today," Augustine teased. "Do you suppose that big bird scared her?"

Beloît grumbled to himself but made no comment.

Pierre enjoyed the wildlife along the river. Red squirrels chattered in the pines and ran along the bank to scold the canoe men. Ducks quacked in the green rice beds, tipping their tails up as they scoured the bottom for food. And birds sang in counterpoint to the *chansons* of the crew.

But what excited the voyageurs most were the many beaver houses. Piled high with fresh aspen cuttings and mud, the lodges hinted that there would be a fine winter of trading ahead. More than once La Petite whistled softly to himself and said, "*Sacré bleu*, this is rich country."

When the brigade reached Lake Vermilion on the following afternoon, they found a perfect campsite in the first bay. A sand beach—rare in that rocky country—stretched for a hundred yards to the west. A ring of blackened stones showed that many campfires had been made here over the years, and the bare frames of abandoned wigwams revealed that an Ojibwe band had recently occupied these shores.

"We may as well camp here, gentlemen," McHenry said, reviewing the map that he'd spread across his knees. "It's a good fifteen miles yet to Windy Point."

"Aye, sir," La Petite replied.

After supper McHenry sat longer than usual with the men. Pierre could tell that everyone was glad to be nearing the place where they would build their trading post. La Petite had finished telling about a winter he'd spent at Cumberland House, when Louie asked how far Cumberland was from York Factory. La Petite deferred to McHenry, saying, "You know the route, sir. What would you guess the distance to be?"

"Close to five hundred miles, I'd say," McHenry replied as he got up to retire to his tent.

But Louie stopped him by asking, "Is that the country where you got your hands scarred, sir?"

"No, son," McHenry gave a crooked smile. "That happened back on Lake Champlain years and years ago."

Louie then asked the question that had long been on Pierre's mind: "What sort of accident was it?"

"It wasn't an accident," McHenry said. Resigned to telling his story, he stepped back toward the fire. "I was only fifteen at the time and out duck hunting by myself when a Mohawk band ambushed me. A Mohawk woman who'd just lost her son adopted me, and I lived with her family for a year. They treated me fair enough and helped me learn the customs of the tribe, but I still wasn't much better than a slave. One night I escaped with an Algonquin fellow they'd captured in a raid. We didn't get far before they tracked us down. They killed the Algonquin on the spot, but a fellow who'd hated me all along had bigger plans for me. He tied me to a tree, and started things off by driving a red hot sword through my foot." McHenry winced involuntarily.

"Next they pulled out my fingernails one at a time. And as if that weren't enough, they shoved my bloody finger tips into a bucket of hot coals." McHenry held his deformed fingers out in the firelight, and Pierre shuddered at the pain he must have felt.

"But just when I thought I was a goner, my adopted mother came along. She threw her arms around me and pleaded for them to stop. For a moment I was afraid they were going to harm her, too, but they didn't. Six months later I escaped for good."

The men sat in silence. Even Beloît made no jokes. So all the stories Pierre had heard about McHenry were true. Pierre stared at the scars on the commander's fingers.

"Enough of this dark talk," McHenry finally said. "Where's your pipe, Augustine? It's time we celebrate our arrival at Vermilion."

"Here, sir," Augustine replied, reaching into his pack.

And in a moment, the voyageurs were dancing to an old French folk tune.

Just before dawn the next morning Pierre was lying half awake when a loon called. He got up from his blanket and walked to the shore. The sky in the east was a smoky red from the fire that was smoldering back at Saganaga. The pungent scent of pine mingled with a warm, marshy smell that drifted up from the river. Though the Vermilion River had been a brownish color from the tannic acid that leached from the bogs and swamps, the waters of Lake Vermilion were clear.

Pierre smiled as he watched a loon swim along the shore less than twenty feet away. The water was so still that a perfect V wake trailed out from the adult's body, and two fluff-balled babies followed behind. When a man up in the camp coughed, the baby loons popped up on the adult's back.

Knowing they had a short paddle today, the rest of the crew woke well after sunrise. The men even tidied themselves up a bit, since they would be bartering for a site to build their winter post. Augustine shaved his head with special care, and a few of the men borrowed combs from a pack of trade goods to smooth their wild locks. "What you prettyin' yourselves up for, fellas?" Beloît asked. "A pig in a poke is still a pig, you know."

They boarded their canoes and set a leisurely pace up a bay that opened gradually into the main body of Vermilion. "Muskego Point lies down there," La Petite waved to the west, "and further on is the Ojibwe village at Wakemup Bay."

By midmorning it was stifling hot, and swarms of horseflies buzzed around the canoes. As Pierre paddled, the sweat ran down his bare back and arms. When Louie complained about the heat, La Petite said, "Enjoy the sunshine while you can, Squeaks. Summer only lasts a few weeks this far north. Some years it hardly comes at all."

"I'd sooner see a blizzard than this blasted heat," Louie insisted.

Beloît laughed from the bow. "Don't never say such things. I've seen it snow in August up here."

"You're joking," Louie scoffed.

"Before you know it, you'll be up to your ears in snowdrifts and begging for spring to come," La Petite said.

Pierre watched Louie shrug. It was clear he didn't believe the old-timers.

The men paddled through a winding channel called Oak Narrows and stopped for breakfast on an island where Beloît claimed the Ojibwe sometimes found gold nuggets. "They call this Gold Island for good reason," he said. "I met a brave up on Rainy Lake who had a fat lump of gold in a leather pouch that he hung around his neck. He said he found that nugget right here."

Pierre looked at the rocky island. Other than a handful of white pines, the vegetation was just straggly ferns and a few stunted oaks.

Augustine knelt and scraped a clump of moss aside, revealing a bluish rock that was streaked with sparkling swirls of white. "There's quartz here," he said. "That's gold-bearing rock for sure. But how a man could ever bust it out of this granite would be another story."

Ignoring Augustine, Beloît continued. "I warned the fellow to stash that nugget away, but he said, 'It's my *manitou*. It gives me special protection.' Later that week someone slit his throat in his sleep." Beloît paused and whispered, "Some protection."

Surprised by the sympathetic tone in Beloît's voice, Pierre turned toward him. But by then Beloît's eyes were lit by an evil glitter. "Just like that." He chuckled darkly and drew his finger across his throat. "There's no magic that can save a man from cold steel." Then he poked Pierre and Louie in the ribs and cackled, "Ain't that right, sweethearts?"

As the day drew on, they paddled past long green islands and towering pines that stood rooted on rock ledges bare of all but the merest trace of soil, and they passed boulder-strewn points where gulls napped in the hot sun. But try as he might to focus on the beauty of the country, Pierre couldn't shake the image of the dead man's necklace. Once when he felt the sharp prick of a fly bite on his neck, he wondered if the man had still been alive to feel the pain when the thief ripped the rawhide off his neck.

La Petite started a song: *"La belle Lisette, chantait l'autre jour..."*

Pierre joined in. He wondered what sort of reception the local band would give them. The Ojibwe on the main canoe routes were used to dealing with the French, but Pierre's father had warned him that the more isolated tribes could be suspicious of traders. "If you treat them right, they'll return the favor," he advised, "but beware if you don't."

When they sighted Windy Point, the commander pulled on his long coat. "I'd better get on my meeting clothes if we're going to negotiate our winter lodgements."

The point was two or three miles long and timbered with a mix of birch and pine and maple. A series of three small islands protected its north side. Pierre could see smoke rising from a campfire in a sandy cove. A group of children were playing along the shore where several well-worn paths led into the forest.

A little girl was the first to notice the approaching canoes. When she called out, more people appeared. By the time the canoes reached the beach, several dozen Ojibwe had gathered to greet the men.

The peacefulness of the scene impressed Pierre. Unlike the rowdy camp back at Grand Portage, which was always filled with oaths and yapping dogs and even gunshots, this sun-drenched shore was calm and orderly.

As McHenry climbed out of the canoe, Pierre caught the smell of birch smoke and roast venison. A man stepped forward. He wore a breech clout, moccasins, and leggings that extended from his ankles to his knees. He was more than six feet tall, and when he raised his hand in greeting, the muscles in his forearm rippled. "My name is Nathaniel Goodsky," he said in French. His hair was cut straight across his forehead, and double braids hung down his back. "I am the chief of the Vermilion band." His profile reminded Pierre of a hawk. Though his dark eyes studied McHenry, his face gave no hint of emotion.

"I am William McHenry," the commander began. "You speak excellent French."

"The missionaries at Sault Sainte Marie taught me, as I have taught my own son, Red Loon." He gestured toward a boy to his right who looked to be about Pierre's age. "I was orphaned when I was only five, and the people at the mission raised me. When I was nine, an aunt from the Vermilion band brought me here."

"You've done well," McHenry said. "We have come from twice as far as the Sault. Our home is a city called Lachine near Montréal. It is our hope to build a trading post on your lake."

"Before we talk business," Goodsky said, "I must tell you of a dream I had."

"Of course," McHenry nodded respectfully.

"It came to me last night, as clear as a face in the noonday sun. I saw two canoes that looked just like these two you now paddle. In the first canoe rode a man who looked very much like you. He wore a fine blue coat with long tails and buttons of bright brass just like these." Goodsky touched a button on the commander's coat as he spoke. "The man in my dream took off his coat and gave it to me as a gift. I told him it was far too generous, but he insisted."

Beloît whispered, "He's a smart one."

McHenry's cheeks flushed as he took off his coat and offered it to the chief. Goodsky thanked McHenry. Then he put the coat on over his bare chest and turned to his people with a smile. The Ojibwe gathered around and touched the fine-spun cloth.

"Perhaps we can now talk of a place for our..." McHenry began, but the chief cut him off.

"It is proper to talk of such matters after we share a meal, William McHenry. We will feast together tomorrow. For now I suggest you camp there." He pointed across the channel to a small island only a few hundred yards away. "We call it Daisy Island."

Then the chief was gone. As McHenry turned, he winked at Pierre. Pierre frowned. Why was the commander winking? After paddling all these weeks, they were being dismissed like disobedient children, yet he was grinning as if he'd just played a clever trick.

The men were silent over supper, and McHenry retired to his tent without a word of his plans for the next day. Later, as Pierre turned restlessly in his blankets, he was furious with McHenry. The campsite the chief had recommended was hot and mosquito infested. Though the men heaped green leaves on the fire to make a smudge, it did little good. Had the commander read so many books that he'd addled his brain? What would the fellow do tomorrow? Make the chief a present of their canoes?

## Chapter Ten

# Windy Point

The men woke up grumpy. The air was stagnant, and clouds of mosquitoes hummed all around them. "I've never seen 'em this big," Beloît grumbled, slapping his forearm and then his thigh. "I swear there's enough meat on these critters to make a stew."

"Don't give Bellegarde any ideas for a new recipe," McHenry spoke from the doorway of his tent. "This is going to be grand country for our trading post."

"And how do you figure on getting the land to build your post?" Beloît asked. "You gonna trade your pants?"

Though the crew laughed, Pierre could see real worry in their faces. If McHenry proved to be a poor leader, they would have no chance for a successful trading season.

After a glum breakfast, McHenry announced, "It's time to call on our neighbors." Dressed in gray knee breeches and a white linen shirt with puffy sleeves, McHenry looked out of place in the wilderness. He could have been a courtier preparing for an audience with the queen.

McHenry took a single canoe and small crew, including Pierre, back to the Ojibwe village. As they neared the beach, a large wolf-like dog ran barking to the water's edge. "He'd make a fine sled dog," Beloît said.

Pierre could see that there was a bigger crowd gathered today. Along with the chief and several men and boys, there were a dozen women. They wore deerskin dresses that were decorated with delicate beading and porcupine quills. They approached the shore with lowered eyes, their children clinging to their sides. How different these ladies looked from the Indian women at Grand Portage, who dressed in calico and put brass rings on their arms and tied bells around their ankles.

Goodsky greeted McHenry as the commander stepped from his canoe. The chief was dressed in McHenry's coat, and he was smiling. "*Bonjour*, William McHenry," Goodsky began. "Welcome once again to Windy Point. I would like to… "

"If you'll excuse me, Chief," McHenry interrupted. Everyone turned toward the commander, astonished at his rudeness. "I must tell you of a wondrous dream that I had last night."

This had better be good, Pierre thought, studying the angry eyes of the chief. "The vision came to me as clear as the light of this fine morning." McHenry paused and waved toward the eastern sky. "In my dream I arrived on a point that looked very much like this one, and I was greeted by a noble brave who looked remarkably like you. In fact, he was wearing a blue coat, just like yours. And when I reached out in my dream to shake his hand, he offered my brigade a fine piece of land on which to build a trading post."

Goodsky's face was stern as he contemplated the commander's words. Finally the chief spoke slowly. "This is a powerful vision, William McHenry," he said, touching the commander's shoulder. "I will show you a place worthy of such a dream."

"Haw, haw," Beloît laughed, startling both McHenry and the chief who were reaching out to shake hands. Then to Pierre's astonishment, Beloît clapped Goodsky on the shoulder and said, "He sure got you there, didn't he, Chief?"

Would they all be killed? Surely Beloît had gone too far this time. But he wasn't done. Next Beloît turned to Goodsky's son, Red Loon, and tousled his hair. "Look's like the talking's done, Loon Boy," he said. "Would you happen to know of any unattached *mesdemoiselles* in these parts?"

Shocked, Red Loon opened his mouth to speak, but Beloît cut him off. "Now there's a gal to match a bold man's dreams," Beloît sang out. "Bless my stars—I'm in love."

Pierre stared as Beloît trotted over to a tall Ojibwe woman. In a jumbled mix of French and Ojibwe, Beloît managed to ask her if she had a husband. When she finally shook her head, Beloît clapped his hands and yelled, "It's my lucky day!" Then he did a little dance in the sand.

"She's a bit broad in the beam for my taste," Augustine chuckled, "but the man sure is smitten."

By now Red Loon was smiling, and he turned to Pierre. "That's my widowed aunt," he said.

"I'm sorry Beloît is so forward," Pierre replied, "but ..."

"No need to apologize," Red Loon said. "Gaazhagens, or Little Cat as you would call her, hasn't smiled since her husband died two summers ago."

Pierre looked at Beloît. A group of women had clustered around the bowman to get a closer look at his scarred face. They were pointing at his torn nose and whispering. Beloît rolled his eyes back in his head and made silly faces that had them all giggling. "*Je suis l'homme*," he crowed.

Goodsky, who was clearly fascinated by Beloît's odd behavior, spoke to McHenry. "Your friend can scramble the cords of his face at will."

"That's not all that's scrambled," McHenry smiled.

# Chapter Eleven

# Bastille Day

Since the next day was July 14th, Bastille Day, McHenry declared a full day off in honor of the French holiday. The men rested through the morning, smoking their pipes and telling stories. In the afternoon the commander told Bellegarde to tap a rum keg. The crew toasted McHenry for the clever way he'd turned events in their favor yesterday. Then they began celebrating.

Late in the afternoon Goodsky and his son paddled out to the island. "We should discuss a site for your post, William McHenry," Goodsky said. He eyed the frolicking crewmen.

"You'll have to excuse my men, but ..." McHenry began.

"I know something of your customs."

While Goodsky retired to McHenry's tent, Red Loon visited with Pierre. Though Beloît offered Red Loon a cup of rum, he politely shook his head.

"You don't know what you're missing, Loon Feather," Beloît called from the rowdy bunch around the fire.

"My father forbids us to take liquor," Red Loon spoke slowly and chose his words with care. "As a young man,

Father saw so many lives destroyed by strong drink that he won't allow it in our village. Though some may sneak a dram—my uncle among them—nearly everyone supports his judgment."

"I understand," Pierre nodded.

"So, what is this Bastille Day, as you call it?" Red Loon asked.

While the voyageurs slugged down their double rations of rum, Pierre tried to explain the history of the Bastille to Red Loon. "It was a huge prison in Paris," Pierre said. "Hundreds of men were locked up though they hadn't broken any laws. The French Revolution began on the day the Bastille was stormed and the men were freed."

Red Loon frowned. He asked what prisons were and where Paris was located. Then he concluded, "It seems silly to worry about such a faraway tribe."

At first Pierre laughed, but the more he thought about it, the more he had to agree. During his time at Grand Portage the previous summer, Pierre had learned that life in the north was occupied with tasks at hand like filling a berry basket and catching a trout. What had happened long ago and far away was unimportant. Like the ancient Epicureans whom Sister had taught him about, the Ojibwe lived according to the philosophy of *carpe diem*, or "seize the day." They planned for the next season, but they relished the present moment without worry.

The next morning the men moved their camp to the mainland and began the job of clearing the land for their trading post. Goodsky had chosen a stand of red pine just above the sandy cove where the brigade first landed. The trees were straight and tall—ideal for cabin logs—and there was a level building site. As a bonus, the beach offered a perfect landing for their canoes.

The men cut the underbrush and saplings first, tossing them onto a huge bonfire. While the older crewmen felled the pines, Louie and Pierre were given the dirty job of peeling off the bark. Working with two-handled drawknives from dawn to dark, the two boys spent the next week covered with pine sap.

Since they worked at the shaded edge of the clearing, mosquitoes pestered them until midmorning. With the coming of the sun, deer flies arrived to chew on them. Pierre soon had pitch smeared all over himself from trying to scratch his bugbites.

"I guess we gotta let the bugs eat what they want of us," Louie said.

To make matters worse, a hot, humid spell settled in. From the moment Pierre picked up his drawknife in the morning until the time he was called for supper, a river of sweat trickled down his back.

"I feel like someone's poured swamp water down my pants," Louie complained.

"Don't give Beloît any ideas," Pierre warned.

One afternoon Pierre took off his cap during a pipe break, and it stuck fast to his sap-covered hand. Beloît called, "What's the matter, pup, is your hat trying to bite you?"

Once the logs were peeled for the trading post, the men set four grooved logs upright for the corners. Then the ends of the wall logs were shaped into splines and slid into place. It was dangerous rolling the logs up angled poles and fitting the splines into the grooves before dropping them into place. Beloît was almost killed one afternoon when a rope broke and the butt end of a log just missed his head. The green logs were heavy to work with, but they were so big that it took only six of them to make a seven-foot wall.

By quitting time, the sharp scent of pine had penetrated Pierre's skin, hair, and clothes. No matter how hard he scrubbed, there was no way to clean the amber goo off his body. Awake or asleep, the pungent odor of pine burned his nostrils.

At night the crew followed the same routine they had since they'd left Montréal last May. The men slept under the shelter of their canoes, while McHenry retired to his tent. Sometimes when Pierre woke late in the night, the Commander's candle was still lit. Pierre wondered what sort of reading or writing kept him up so late. But no matter how late the candle burned, McHenry always rose early and never showed a hint of fatigue.

To escape the clouds of mosquitos that hovered under the overturned canoes, Pierre and Louie often laid their blankets beside the campfire and slept in the open. Then they put green cedar boughs on the coals and set up a smudge.

One evening after supper, Augustine told a story about a shipwreck he'd survived in the Azores. When he was done, McHenry turned to Pierre. "Speaking of shipwrecks," he said, "have you read *Robinson Crusoe*?"

"Yes, sir."

"Then let me show you something." The commander led Pierre to his tent. McHenry's journal lay open on a rough-hewn plank that was supported by two wooden crates. Beside his journal was an inkwell and a quill pen. "I've been keeping a journal since 1789," he said. "I haven't missed a day in the last twelve years."

McHenry's library was lined up on two half-log shelves in the rear of the tent. The spines of the rich, leather-bound volumes were lettered in gold. Stepping up to the shelf, he said, "Here it is," and handed him a slim brown volume.

Pierre looked at the title, *The Life and Strange, Surprising Adventures of Robinson Crusoe*, and opened the book. "But this is in English," Pierre said. Assuming McHenry had picked the wrong book he handed it back to the commander. Though Pierre knew a little English, all his schoolwork had been in French or Latin.

"If you want to advance with the North West

Company," McHenry said, "knowing a bit of English really helps. Nearly all the partners are Brits or Scots."

"I know." Pierre stopped and stared at the book. "But how could I ever read something this long?"

"You know the story, right?"

"Yes, but ..."

"Have a seat, then." McHenry motioned toward a keg. "I'll get you started."

Pierre was surprised at how rapidly the cabin building progressed. The long summer days allowed the men to start at five each morning, and the sky was still bright at nine in the evening. The voyageurs did their log work at the same frantic pace with which they portaged and paddled. "The faster we go," La Petite declared, "the sooner we sleep with a roof over our heads."

Once the walls were in place, the men cut rafters from spruce trees in a nearby swamp. Cedar bark finished off the roof, and the walls were chinked with a mixture of mud, sphagnum moss, and ashes. Though it was extra work, McHenry insisted on a puncheon floor, made of split logs pegged in place over the hard-packed dirt. A log chimney lined with clay and windows made of oiled deerskin finished things off.

Many Ojibwe visited the voyageurs' camp to watch them work, and Pierre got to know several of the men and boys. His favorite was Red Loon, who was curious about the trading post and anxious to practice his French.

If Ojibwe women stopped by camp, Beloît dropped his tools to flirt. They called him the "One Who Makes His Face Dance" and giggled loudly whenever he turned his eyelids inside out or pulled his lip up over his nose. The other men were jealous when Beloît got all the attention, but they knew there was no competing with what André called his "rare idiot talent."

Each evening McHenry guided Pierre through the English version of Robinson Crusoe. Pierre stumbled at first, but as he read the book out loud, he discovered that many English words had Latin roots that he'd learned in school. Before long, he was reading so well that McHenry could write in his journal and correct Pierre's occasional mistakes at the same time.

Beloît teased Pierre about his English lessons, saying "Where's your chalk and slate, schoolboy?" or "Too bad your Mama isn't here to pack a lunch for you." But Pierre ignored him. Not only did he believe McHenry was right about the importance of English, but he also loved Robinson Crusoe's story. Once Pierre got to the part where the shipwrecked sailor found a mysterious footprint in the sand, nothing could keep him from finishing the tale.

# Chapter Twelve

# The Sweat Lodge

On July 31, 1801, the brigade celebrated the completion of their first building, a log storehouse for trade goods. The voyageurs and Ojibwe gathered in front of the split log door while McHenry made a speech.

"I'd like to thank our Ojibwe friends for their generosity in sharing this rich land ..." As the commander spoke, Pierre noticed that Beloît, who was standing off to the side, had loaded his Northwest gun and was leaning a ladder against the gable end of the building. Then, winking at Pierre and putting his finger to his lips, Beloît climbed onto the roof.

Though Pierre didn't say a word, in a short while everyone was staring up at Beloît. "What in the blazes is going on?" McHenry said, stopping his speech and stepping back from the building to see for himself. When he saw Beloît on the roof he couldn't help grinning.

"Beloît stood up and shouted, *"Vive Napoléon!"* discharging his musket at the same time. The kick of the gun tipped him backwards, and when he planted a moccasin to steady himself, he slipped. Everyone's mouth dropped open as he skidded out of sight down the back of the roof.

Augustine was the first one to reach Beloît. "What a lucky fool," Augustine laughed. For Beloît had pitched headlong off the roof and landed in a pile of sawdust and wood chips, narrowly missing an axe and a chopping block.

Beloît looked up and mumbled, "*Je suis l'homme.*"

The following Sunday, the only day of the week the voyageurs were free to do as they pleased, Red Loon approached Pierre, "My father asked if you would come to our sweat lodge."

"Sweat lodge?" Pierre asked.

"The sweat lodge purifies us in both body and mind."

When they reached the village, a half dozen boys and girls were playing a game of hide-and-seek. One little girl was running in a circle. She was holding her nose and calling out, "*Memengwe, memengwe.*"

"What's she doing?" Pierre asked.

"Calling butterflies," Red Loon laughed. "It may sound strange, but they seem to come."

The children ran up to Red Loon. The smallest girl tugged at his hand and asked him something. But he shook his head.

"What does she want?" Pierre asked, seeing how disappointed she was.

"It's nothing." Red Loon shrugged. "They want to play a silly game."

"I don't mind," Pierre said.

"Really?" Red Loon stopped. The small ones were already jumping up and down with joy.

Pierre nodded.

"Follow me," Red Loon said.

The two boys walked up the hill. Red Loon paused by a clump of hazel brush. He took out his knife and cut a handful of leafy branches that he stuck all around his headband. All Pierre could see were eyes and teeth through the dark leaves.

Pierre chuckled. "Are you trying to disguise yourself as a tree?"

"Don't laugh." Red Loon smiled. "You're next."

"Oh, no," Pierre protested.

"You said you'd play," Red Loon insisted, cutting more branches and tying them around Pierre's head with a rawhide thong. Then Red Loon picked up a stick and led Pierre to a cedar thicket. They crouched in the shadow of a broad tree.

A moment later the Ojibwe children appeared, walking single file and peering cautiously from side to side. When they were only a few paces away, Red Loon leaped up. He brandished the stick over his head and let out a shriek.

The children squealed and scattered in all directions. Red Loon ran after the little girl who'd been so anxious to play. He picked her up and pretended to bite her middle.

As she screamed and giggled, the other children ran back and pretended to hit Red Loon with sticks. Then Red Loon and Pierre chased the children, alternately attacking and retreating, and taking care not to scare the little ones too much.

After a while Red Loon declared the game was over. "My father is waiting," he said, "but we will play another day."

Red Loon brought Pierre to the far end of the village. Goodsky and an older man were kneeling over a fire. Behind them stood a blanket-covered framework of bent poles. They were heating round rocks on the coals. Red Loon said, "This is my uncle, Waawaashkeshi noondaa' gozigan."

Pierre's eyes widened. How could he ever remember such a name? Red Loon smiled and said, "His name means 'One who is skilled at calling like a deer,' but you can just call him Uncle."

Goodsky and Waawaashkeshi both nodded to Pierre, but neither man spoke as they lifted three small stones with antlers and carried them into the lodge. When they returned for the largest stone, Red Loon's uncle said, "Be careful the grandfather does not fall."

When Pierre frowned, Red Loon said, "The big stone is called the grandfather, because the steam that rises from it carries our songs to the Creator." Then Red Loon motioned toward the lodge. "It is time." The men, who had already stripped to their breechclouts, stepped inside. Red Loon and Pierre took off their clothes and followed.

It was dark and warm in the lodge. The blanket-covered frame was less than four feet in diameter, and the shoulders of the men nearly touched as they sat in a circle around the hot stones. Goodsky lit a pipe and drew in two deep puffs before passing it on to Uncle, who did the same. Though Pierre didn't smoke, when his turn came he pulled politely on the pipe and was surprised to taste sweet willow bark instead of tobacco. The air was hot, and the smoke clouded Pierre's eyes.

No one spoke until the pipe was returned to Goodsky. Then the chief dipped a bunch of grass into a water basin and sprinkled it on the largest stone. Beads of sweat gathered on Pierre's forehead as the steam rose. Goodsky sang a song, and the other men repeated part of it three times in a soft, musical rhythm.

When the song was over, the grass was handed to the uncle, who sprinkled more water on the stone and spoke as the steam rose: "May the Creator's healing breath bring us long and healthy lives." Then the song was repeated.

When the grass and water basin were handed to Pierre, he wondered what he might say. His head felt light, and his cheeks burned from the heat. What was proper? What might dishonor the occasion? He sprinkled the water on the stone and said simply, "May the fire never die." The words must have been fitting, for Goodsky nodded politely before he began the final song.

After a moment of silence, Red Loon's uncle lifted the

blanket from the doorway, and the men stepped outside. As they wiped the sweat from their faces and shared a drink of water, the uncle said, "Your friend speaks well, Red Loon. You must invite him to our wigwam this winter to share our stories."

Later, when Red Loon walked Pierre back to the Post, he explained what his uncle meant. "According to custom we only tell our stories when there is ice on the lakes and snow on the ground. It is a great honor to be invited. I'm sure your people have many fine stories that you can share with us."

That night as Pierre drifted off to sleep, he was wondering what sort of story he could possibly tell an Ojibwe chief. Cinderella? A Bible story like Noah's Ark? His eyes and throat still burned from the pipe smoke, but his body felt clean and light. Even the pine pitch had been loosened from his hands. Something in the ceremony reminded him of the power he'd felt during his First Communion. Was it a sin to compare Father Michael's silver chalice to the sweet grass and smoke of the sweat lodge?

Two weeks later, Red Loon invited Pierre to go on a short canoe trip with his father and uncle. "They want to inspect the wild rice crop that grows in the marsh at the end of the bay," Red Loon said. "We call the rice *Maanoomin*."

"I know," Pierre nodded, remembering last summer's feast in Kennewah's wigwam.

"Then you know it is our most important food, a gift that saves us from starving when hard winters make game scarce."

Once again McHenry was pleased to let Pierre go with the Ojibwe. "A poor rice crop can mean trouble for us all," he said.

Though they took Ojibwe canoes that morning, Pierre brought his own paddle. When he arrived at the beach, Red Loon's uncle pointed at him and laughed, "*Ikweabwi!*"

Uncle took Pierre's short voyageur paddle from his hand. "*Ikweabwi* means woman's paddle," Red Loon said, as Uncle stood Pierre's paddle beside his own. It was nearly twice as wide and much longer.

While Red Loon went to get another paddle for Pierre, Uncle was still laughing. He said something in Ojibwe that Goodsky translated as, "Can't you handle a man-sized paddle? Or did you paddle so hard that you wore that one down?"

As soon as Pierre got into Red Loon's canoe, he could see the advantage of the Ojibwe paddle. By pulling deeply and slowly, he and Red Loon could propel this light craft faster than a half dozen voyageurs could paddle a north canoe.

Skimming across the water in silence—the Ojibwe didn't sing when they paddled—Pierre and Red Loon followed closely behind the lead canoe. When they arrived in a shallow bay a half hour later, Goodsky and his brother shipped their paddles. "Though we mainly rice in a lake south of here," Red Loon said, "this patch helps us judge the potential of the harvest."

The uncle reached for a stalk of wild rice and pulled the tufted head over the canoe. He crumpled the rice grains into his open palm. Choosing one, he peeled off the outer sheath to check the kernel underneath. It was green and produced a milky fluid when Uncle broke it. Repeating the process, he shook his head. When he finally spoke, his words sounded like a slow, sad song.

"It's worse than they thought," Red Loon explained to Pierre. "The rice stand is thin, and that storm we had last week knocked down much of what was growing. It will be a meager harvest this year."

"But there's plenty of game," Pierre said.

"For now there is plenty of everything, but the deep snows are coming soon."

# Chapter Thirteen

# Manitou

The Windy Point Trading Post was completed in early October. Along with the storehouse, the men had built a cabin for Commander McHenry and a bunkhouse for themselves. Pierre was disappointed when McHenry left his tent for his new lodgings. Pierre had gotten used to the slender figure of the commander silhouetted against the tent wall at night. He and McHenry had talked almost every evening over the last few weeks. Would they visit as often now?

As soon as the last building was finished, the commander invited Goodsky and his people over to celebrate. The voyageurs spitted two venison haunches over the coals of a big fire, and Bellegarde served liquor rations all around. Though the Ojibwe enjoyed the food, they politely refused the liquor, with the exception of Little Cat and Waawaashkeshi.

Beloît soon got "rummed up" and made a fool of himself by dancing a jig with his eyes crossed. The women laughed and laughed when they saw that as Beloît drank more rum, his eyes were slower and slower to uncross.

Beloît invited Little Cat to dance, asking, "How about a

spin, Kitten?"

Winking at Pierre, he whispered, "Dance 'em before you romance 'em, La Page. They can't resist a little lovin' after a quick whirl around the fire." Pierre blushed at this bad conduct, but Goodsky and Red Loon only laughed.

To make matters worse, as Beloît danced, he let out an occasional "Meow," which made Little Cat and the other Ojibwe women giggle. Though most of the voyageurs ignored his idiocy, Augustine was peeved.

"What's the use of me piping a tune with all that caterwauling, Jean Beloît?" he shouted.

"You make your music, Auggie, and I'll make mine." Beloît kicked his legs high and let out another screech.

One morning Red Loon stopped by the post and invited Pierre to go on an overnight trip to scout for game.

"I'll have to ask the commander," Pierre said, continuing to work on the snowshoe frame he was fitting together.

After Red Loon watched Pierre work for a few more minutes, he said, "Aren't you going to ask him?"

"How soon do you plan on going?"

"Today."

Pierre grinned. He was always amazed at how quickly Red Loon acted once he had made up his mind.

When he asked permission, the commander said, "That would be a good idea, son. It's wise to learn the lay of the land before the trading season begins."

Pierre and Red Loon left later that morning. As they hiked along the well-worn path that led off Windy Point, Pierre asked, "Would you have gone by yourself if I hadn't been able to come?"

"Of course," Red Loon said. "My father often challenges me to test my woods skills."

"Do you always travel this light?" Red Loon carried only a small leather sack, his knife, and his bow. Pierre had a pack on his back stuffed with his blanket and provisions.

"Sometimes I carry less. Last year Father blackened my

face and sent me into the woods for a week. I fasted day and night, taking only a little water to keep up my strength."

"But why?"

"Before a boy becomes a man, he must seek a dream. Fasting lightens the mind so that it can see ..."

Red Loon stopped suddenly. He raised his hand to signal for silence.

Pierre listened for a long time before he heard anything. Then came a scraping sound followed by a low grunt. Red Loon waved for Pierre to follow. They stalked up an aspen ridge, stepping only in the mossy places where their moccasins would make no noise.

By the time they reached the top of the ridge, the grunting and scraping was twice as loud. Kneeling in the shadow of a large balsam, Red Loon pointed into the swale and whispered, "Look."

Pierre could see a dark patch, and then suddenly a head with an enormous rack of antlers appeared. "A moose!" Pierre said. "If only I'd brought my rifle."

The huge beast was raking his antlers up and down a tree trunk. Then the moose lowered his head and charged into a rotten aspen that was riddled with woodpecker holes. Pierre winced as the bull hit the tree with a loud crack. To his amazement, the tree shivered and fell. Dust rose from the dry leaves.

The moose pawed the ground. Then suddenly he stopped.

"He's scented us," Red Loon said. "Watch this." He stood up and whistled and waved his arms.

Pierre's eyes went wide. What if the big bull charged?

Pierre looked for cover, but the moose snorted once and plunged into the brush. "They have great noses, but they don't see so well," Red Loon laughed. "He'll probably run all the way to Lost Lake."

"Where's that?"

Red Loon pointed across a huge swamp. "Over there, a good two miles beyond the muskeg."

Pierre walked over to the tree the moose had knocked down. It was at least eight inches thick and had cracked into three pieces when it fell. Pierre picked up a bright feather from the leaves. "Look at this," he said.

The feather was a soft russet color. It was about six inches long and had a dark band with a splash of white on the tip. Pierre held it out to Red Loon.

"This is a strong sign," he said. "Perhaps it is your *manitou*? We will show it to my father when we return."

"*Manitou* is like a good luck charm?" Pierre asked, slipping the feather into his pack.

"More than that," Red Loon said. "It's a token for special protection." Pierre thought back to Beloît's story of the brave who'd had his throat slit for a gold nugget. Did he want such a charm?

Pierre and Red Loon hiked north along the shore of Vermilion and made camp on a rocky ridge that overlooked the lake. "We call this Sunset Rock," Red Loon said. "My cousins and I have come here since we were small. The berry picking and hunting are fine in these hills. And in that creek over there, we spear northerns this big in the spring." He spread his hands a yard apart and smiled.

For supper they walked down to the shore and caught two bass with a hand line. When Pierre drew out his knife to fillet the fish, Red Loon admired La Londe's carving on the handle, and Pierre told him about the day his old friend had saved a canoe full of men.

As the boys roasted their fish over an open fire, they laughed and joked as if they had known each other for a long time. Just before sunset Red Loon showed Pierre a huge white pine at the top of the ridge. The branches were smooth from the many moccasins that had climbed it. The tree reminded Pierre of a big oak near his home in

Lachine that he and his friends climbed and played under. Father had tied a swing to a stout branch that faced the river. From that seat Pierre could watch the blue St. Lawrence and mark the arrival of the tall ships from the east and the canoe brigades from the west. Pierre wondered what Celeste was doing this evening, so far away. In quiet moments back in Lachine, did Celeste think of him as he was thinking of her tonight?

"Let me show you the view," Red Loon grinned, catching a branch with both hands and pulling himself upward. A minute later the boys had climbed to a limb twenty feet off the ground. Standing up, Red Loon clenched the trunk with one arm and pointed west. "See that bay beyond the hill?" he asked.

Pierre nodded. The air was heavy with pine scent, and a squirrel chattered above their heads.

"When caribou pass through here, that big water forces them to follow the shore, so they always cross somewhere close by."

"I didn't know there were caribou in this country until I saw some running from the wildfire on Knife Lake," Pierre said.

"They range all the way up to Husdon's Bay. Some years the hunts are grand."

After the sun went down, the boys slept in the dried pine needles on top of the ridge. Though Pierre offered to share his blanket with Red Loon, he shook his head. "My deerskin shirt is padding enough," he said.

Pierre was grateful that the mosquitoes were finally gone. And as the coolness of the full dark descended, he fell into a deep, dreamless sleep.

What seemed like only minutes later, Pierre awoke to a terrible shriek. He sat up, shaking. Red Loon was already on his feet. His bow was at full draw, and he was aiming in the direction from which the horrible cry had come.

Pierre drew out his knife. His heart raced as he held his breath. In the moonlight Pierre could see the muscles in

Red Loon's jaw tense as he stared into the shadows, trying to pick out a target for his arrow.

Suddenly there was a laugh in the darkness behind them. Red Loon turned, and there was a second louder laugh on the opposite side. This time Red Loon chuckled, too.

Pierre was confused until a voice boomed in the darkness, "You've done well, my son." Then Goodsky appeared.

After he had shaken Pierre's hand, Goodsky clapped his son on the back and said, "You've shown the readiness of a true warrior." He laughed. "Not like that night we stole your moccasins, eh?"

Red Loon gave a crooked smile and nodded as his uncle stepped out of the shadows and congratulated him, too.

Then as suddenly as the men had appeared, they were gone. "What was all that about?" Pierre asked, still not fully awake. His head throbbed. Had this all been a bad dream?

"I should have warned you," Red Loon said. "The men of the village always test us like this. We must prove that we are ready for a Sioux attack. Sometimes the men give a war cry in the dark to see how fast we react. Other times they sneak up and try to touch us with a coup stick.

"Once when I was very small," Red Loon continued with a smile, "I was camping with my older cousin, and my uncle crept up in the night and stole our moccasins. He teased us for many days. Though it is a game, it is a serious one, for warriors who sleep too soundly may not wake at all."

Pierre wanted to ask more questions, but Red Loon had already lain down and was snoring softly. How could he relax so fast? It took Pierre a long time to quiet the beating of his heart. And throughout the night he found himself waking at the smallest sound. Were the men still out there at the edge of the dark, waiting to trick them again?

When the boys arrived back at the village the next

morning, Goodsky greeted them with a grin. "Did you sleep well?"

After the joking was done, Red Loon showed his father the hawk's feather that Pierre had found. Goodsky took the feather in his hand and touched it to Pierre's head. "With such snowy hair, we must call you White Hawk. That will be your true name from this day forward." Then he stepped into his wigwam and brought out a small leather bag tied to a rawhide cord. "You must keep your *manitou* close to your heart." He put the hawk's feather in the bag and slid the cord over Pierre's head. Pierre fingered the soft leather pouch, feeling for a hint of magic in the charm.

# Chapter Fourteen

# Marie Antoinette

Once the last of the buildings was finished, the daily routine at the post slowed. The cold weather they needed for preserving fish and game was still a few weeks away, and the pelts weren't yet prime for trapping. Stuck between summer and the trading season yet to come, the voyageurs bided their time with simple jobs. They cut and chopped wood, built furniture, made snares, and tied lines for the sled dogs they would be running on trading trips. To get ready for winter, the men also oiled their moccasins and darned the holes in their woolen socks and underwear. One day Augustine sewed himself a pair of deerskin mitts which he held up proudly.

Beloît scoffed and said, "These ones that Little Cat made me are lots better." He reached into his pack and pulled out a pair of white, rabbit skin mitts. The men laughed as he put them on and held up his hands. "Sweet, eh?" he said. "But here's the best part." He drew out a fluffy rabbit skin cap, which he pulled over his ears. Beloît's grimy face and mutilated nose looked so horrible next to the soft, white fur that everyone roared.

"That man is so ugly I'm gonna have nightmares the rest of my days on this earth," Augustine said.

The bright, cool weather was a joy to Pierre. He and Red Loon and Louie hunted squirrels, grouse, and ducks. They hiked along the pine ridge that ran to the end of Windy Point. One day Red Loon showed the boys a deep crater that his people said had been made by a falling star. They marveled at the huge hole.

But no matter how busy Pierre was, he missed home. Back in Lachine autumn was a time to help his mother and sisters pick the last of the apples, to help Father with the butchering, and to stack firewood. Last fall when he'd returned from his first summer with the brigades, he and Celeste had taken long walks beyond the village.

"Monsieur canoeman," she would tease, "are you sure you can travel so far without your paddle?"

"Not only do I not need a paddle, *mademoiselle*," Pierre bragged, "but I could carry you from here to your father's doorstep."

"How bold we have become," she giggled.

Spending a whole year away from home would be more difficult than Pierre had imagined. When the brigade was on the move, he didn't have a chance to be lonesome. But now that time had slowed, his mind turned to home. And the loss of Kennewah and her family haunted him. It was so unfair. Whenever he watched the children playing in the Ojibwe village, he thought of Kennewah lying in a grave house above the dark waters of Lake Superior. Why her? Why them? The questions rocked him to the core.

Pierre was glad to be distracted by preparations for the trading season. McHenry and La Petite taught him how to keep the account book in which all the transactions were recorded. Using a system of pictures, they kept track of the goods the post advanced to each family. McHenry praised Pierre's handwriting, but he teased him about the little symbols he drew. "What's this?" he said, staring at a leghold trap Pierre had drawn. "A set of false teeth?"

"Well, how about my copper kettles?" Pierre asked.

"What do you think, La Petite?" McHenry said, showing him the tiny sketch.

"They look like milk pails to me," La Petite laughed.

Every evening after supper McHenry continued Pierre's English lessons. Pierre had finished *Robinson Crusoe* and was halfway through an English edition of Voltaire's *Candide*. One evening Pierre asked McHenry, "Did Voltaire make up the part where non-believers are punished by being burned alive?"

"They was roasted good, La Page," Beloit hollered, stomping out the door on his way to Little Cat's wigwam. "And the reason they was burned was they asked too many questions! Shouldn't school be out by this late in the day, ladies?"

"There's a fellow who's going to die as ignorant as the day he was born," Pierre muttered.

"Don't be too sure," McHenry said. "He knows more than he's willing to admit."

"Him?" Pierre asked.

When McHenry nodded, Pierre stared at the cackling fool. What could the commander possibly mean?

One day Louie and Bellegarde came back from a hunting trip and said that they needed help dragging a sow bear back to the post. Beloît and Pierre and Augustine all went along.

When they reached the carcass, Pierre was sad to see a bear cub bawling over its dead mother. It ran to the edge of the woods when the men approached but kept crying in the underbrush. To Pierre, it sounded like the little thing was saying "Maaa, Maaa." And when André and Augustine tied the front legs of the bear to a dragging pole, the little critter walked up to the mother and sniffed her. Then it bawled even more loudly.

André cocked his rifle, saying, "The kindest thing we can do is put it in the soup pot."

Pierre turned his head, not wanting to see the cub get shot, but Beloît said, "Put down that gun."

"What?" André said.

"The little tyke deserves better than that."

Pierre couldn't believe his ears. The cruelest man he'd ever met was taking the side of a bear cub! "Come on, little gal," Beloît said, kneeling and taking a bit of venison jerky from his pouch. When the bear snatched the meat from his palm, Beloît smiled. "She's a smart one, but kind of runty for this late in the year."

"How do you know it's a she?" Augustine asked.

"She's too cute to be anything but a lady," Beloît said.

"A cub that small will never survive," André insisted. "Let's do the right thing."

But when he raised his gun again, Beloît clenched his teeth. "Put that down before I bend the barrel around your ears."

"Have it your way," André shrugged and lowered the gun.

The little bear bawled the whole way back to camp, alternately sniffing its dead mother and licking Beloît's hand as it begged for more food. "We'll get you something better when we get home," Beloît said to the cub.

"Home?" André scoffed. "Why don't you stop babying that critter and help us drag this carcass?"

"Shut up," Beloît snapped. "Can't you see she's upset?"

As soon as they got back to the Post, Beloît took some pork fat out of a keg and spooned it onto his tin plate. "Here you go, girl."

He grinned proudly as the bear gobbled down every morsel.

When dinnertime came, Beloît could talk of nothing but

his newfound friend. "Ain't she a little darling?" he said, stepping up to the stew pot to load his plate.

"Did you wash the bear slobber off that plate?" Augustine asked from behind.

"Do you think I'm a pig?" Beloît said.

"We know you're a pig," André said, as Beloît heaped his plate full.

Pierre gagged. He knew that Beloît hadn't wiped his plate off. Just when Beloît had done the grossest thing Pierre thought he possibly could, he did something worse.

As Beloît took a seat and pulled his spoon out, the little bear snuffled up beside him, stuck out her tongue, and lapped half the stew off his plate.

"Look at her," Beloît laughed proudly. "Now that's bad manners. I got a perfect name for you—Marie Antoinette." The men all chuckled, knowing the bad reputation of the recently executed French Queen.

But their laughter stopped when Beloît took a spoonful off the same plate and shoveled it into his mouth.

"I knew it," Augustine moaned. "You are the most revolting pig of a man I've ever seen."

"I can't believe it," Louie groaned, and the rest of the men joined in.

Beloît said, "A fine stew, Bellegarde," as he downed a second spoonful.

# Chapter Fifteen

# A Long Winter's Nap

By the time the birches had shed the last of their golden leaves, nearly all the local Ojibwe had stopped by the post and picked up their trade goods for the season.

One morning after breakfast La Petite looked at the full account book and said, "We'll have a fine take if everyone delivers the furs they've promised."

"What if they don't?" Pierre asked.

"Barring sickness or death, I've never known a native family who didn't follow through. Remember last year when Commander McKay told you that if you give an Ojibwe a trade gun in the fall, you can count on twenty pelts come winter? That's how the system works."

As the youngest crewmen, Pierre and Louie spent most of their time helping André with the food stores. Both boys were amazed at the amount of food that André cached. He smoked venison jerky on wooden racks. He traded with the Ojibwe for dried berries, squash, maple sugar, and what wild rice they could spare. He set nets daily for whitefish and walleyes.

And every one of the fish was cleaned by Pierre and Louie. "Isn't this enough?" Louie whined one afternoon, as he gutted their twentieth-fourth fish, slit its tail, and slid it onto the drying pole.

"We need at least two per day per man to make it through the winter," André insisted.

"But that's hundreds of fish!" Pierre said, multiplying men and days and fish in his head.

"We'll need lots of fuel to keep us going in the cold..." The cook suddenly turned. "Stop that!" he shouted.

Pierre laughed. Beloît's bear, Marie, had sneaked up to the drying pole and was tugging at a fish.

"Get!" the cook yelled at the top of his lungs. He picked up the nearest thing, which happened to be a fat whitefish, and threw it at the bear. The fish hit Marie in the side of the face, and she happily grabbed it in her teeth and dashed toward the woods. Pierre and Louie laughed as André cursed the bear.

By now Marie Antoinette was like a member of the crew. Beloît didn't care how much the men teased him about his pet. He doted on Marie like a proud father, and the little bear followed him wherever he went. Once Beloît even tried coaxing Marie into going for a canoe ride, until McHenry put a stop to it. "We'll not risk damaging a boat to indulge your spoiled baby," he declared.

Though the voyageurs looked on the always hungry bear as a nuisance, the Ojibwe were fascinated by Beloît's attachment to the cub. They began calling Beloît "Father Bear." At first Pierre thought the band was making fun of Beloît, but Red Loon told him the opposite. "The bear is a powerful spirit," he said, "and your friend ..."

"Don't call him my friend."

"Friend or not, he must have a special strength for the bear to choose him as her guardian."

"The bear tolerates him because he feeds her," Pierre said.

"There is more to it than that," Red Loon said.

As Pierre watched Beloît and Marie together, he had to admit that there was something special in their bond. The bear brought out a softer side of Beloît—a side that Pierre had never seen in their two summers together.

An idea came to Beloît after supper one evening. The men had gorged themselves on venison and wild rice and had just settled back to light their pipes. Beloît was chattering at Marie, who had devoured her usual huge portion over André's protests, when Beloît suddenly stopped in mid-sentence.

"What's the matter?" La Petite asked. "Did your little lady friend finally talk back?"

"If she did," Augustine said, "I hope she told him to shut up." The men all laughed.

"She yawned," Beloît said.

"So would you if you sucked down that much food," André said.

"But don't you see what this means? It's fall," Beloît went on, not caring if anyone was listening. "It's time for little *mademoiselle* to take her winter's nap."

Beloît then took up a shovel and began digging a hole at the edge of the woods. The little bear waddled along behind him and sat sniffing at the dirt Beloît piled by the hole.

"You digging for gold?" Louie called.

"Looks like he's starting a rose garden," Augustine said.

"Shut yer yaps," Beloît yelled back. "I'm digging a house for my Marie."

The entire camp, McHenry included, burst into laughter, but Beloît refused to be dissuaded from his task.

Every night after supper for the next three days, he worked at hollowing out a hole for Marie. "You'll sleep pretty here," he said, pausing to scratch the little bear's ears.

When the bear house, as he called it, was finished, he tried to coax Marie into the hole. "Time to sleep," he said, leading her toward the entrance. But she sniffed once at the edge and refused to go inside.

Beloît tried everything. He tossed a bit of maple candy into the den. He crawled into the waist-deep hole himself and said, "Look at what a sweet home I've dug for you." He even tried pushing the pudgy bear down into the hole, but she planted her paws and wouldn't budge.

The whole camp roared. "Maybe she wants you to get her a feather bed?" McHenry called, and the men laughed even more loudly.

In a huff Beloît kicked a clump of dirt into the hole and walked away.

A week later the little bear dug a den of her own right next to Beloît's hole. Then she scraped some dried leaves around the entrance, crawled inside her new home, and went to sleep. Though Beloît stood over the hole and cursed the cub for ignoring his "fine accommodations," Pierre could tell he was proud that Marie was clever enough to make her own winter shelter.

# Chapter Sixteen

# *Gashkadino-Giizis* or Freezing Over Moon

In mid-November, a warm spell caught the traders by surprise. The black skim of ice which had just covered the lake melted away, and for a week a warm breeze blew out of the south. André's smoked venison survived the heat, but all of his fish spoiled.

"It's dog food now," André said after he visited the cache they'd made in the cedars to keep the meat cool.

"So all our work was for nothing?" Louie said.

André nodded. Pierre thought back to the scales and slime the boys had washed off their hands, and the huge mound of fish guts they'd buried.

"We've got to reset our nets," André said, "and hope we can catch enough before the lake refreezes."

The next day they put out the nets again, but the weather took a sudden turn for the worse. An icy wind howled out of the north, and by nightfall the temperature had dropped forty-five degrees.

The next morning Pierre woke feeling as if something was wrong. He lay for a moment until he realized it was the quiet. He had never heard such perfect, unbroken stillness. After slipping on his moccasins, Pierre opened the door. Ten inches of fresh snow had fallen during the night, and more was coming down. The air smelled damp and cold.

"Shut the door," La Petite groaned from his bunk. "Were you raised in a barn?" Pierre put on his woolen capote and pulled the leather-hinged door shut behind him. He stepped out into a world transformed.

Every detail of the landscape had been rounded and softened by the snow. The sharp lines of the benches and roof tops were lost. Pines branches that had been clusters of bright green needles yesterday were now shapeless white clumps.

The cold weather signaled the official beginning of the trading season. The pelts would be prime now, and the snow would allow travel by dogsled. Traders and trappers alike could cover four times the distance they did on foot.

With the coming of winter, Goodsky held true to his promise to share the tribal legends with Pierre. Red Loon visited the post one morning and invited the voyageurs to attended a feast in his father's wigwam. Though Pierre was hoping Beloît wouldn't be included, Red Loon said Little Cat insisted that an invitation be extended to Brave Bear, as she called him.

The sumptuous meal reminded him of the summer when he and La Londe had dined with Makwa at Grand Portage. Red Loon's mother served smoked whitefish, duck boiled with wild rice, fire-baked squash, and fried bread. For dessert she offered roasted hazelnuts and maple candy, followed by bowls of wintergreen tea.

As he sat in the tight circle of men, Pierre thought of Kennewah. How unfair it was that he should be feasting on fine food and drinking sweet tea while she lay in the cold company of the grave house. He recalled, as he had a hundred times, her black, straight-parted hair that glistened in the firelight, her soft doeskin dress and shy smile. What justice could there be in taking such beauty from the world?

After the meal, Goodsky said, "Now that the earth is covered with snow and the lake is sleeping under ice, the time has come to share the strength of our legends with you."

"There's nothing like a good yarn to pass a winter's night," Beloît said. Pierre was embarrassed, but Goodsky only smiled politely.

The chief told a story of three men who went on a quest to meet Winabojo, the master of life. Each of the men hoped that Winabojo, a master trickster, would use his great powers to grant him a wish.

"After journeying for many days and enduring many hardships," Goodsky said, "the men arrived at the wigwam of Winabojo. Thinking that the great master would be quick to grant their requests, the boldest man stepped forward and said, 'Great one, I ask that you grant me the gift of eternal life.'

"In scorn Winabojo picked up the man and threw him into the corner, where he was turned into a black stone. 'Now you will last as long as the earth,' he declared.

"The second spoke with more care. 'Noble Winabojo, lord of all the universe, I ask that you give me the gift of wisdom and cleverness.'

"'Be it so,' said Winabojo, and with a wave of his hand he turned the man into a raven that flapped away, croaking in the dry wind.

"The last man, knowing he must put all hope of personal gain aside, said, 'I humbly ask that you give me the power to heal my people.'

"Winabojo leaped up from his seat. The man trembled. But then the Lord of All Things smiled and handed him a medicine bag and a red sash. 'Take these,' he said, 'and be forever blessed.'

"'And as a further reward I offer you my daughter's hand in marriage, so that the happiness you bring to others will also be multiplied unto yourself.'"

"Ha, Ha," Beloît winked at Little Cat.

The chief concluded with a quiet nod and said, "Now perhaps one of our friends might share a tale of their people?"

Beloît poked Pierre in the ribs, shouting, "How about La Page here. He's a walking dictionary if there ever was one. Tell us all a story, Pierre."

Pierre blushed. Why didn't this fool ever keep his mouth shut? Everyone turned toward Pierre and waited. He searched his mind for a myth or legend that might be fitting. He could think of nothing that would compare with Goodsky's poetic tale.

"What's the matter, La Page?" Beloît said, "Is your head so jumbled with schoolbook nonsense that you can't talk?"

Pierre began slowly, having no idea which story to tell. "I remember a tale that Sister told our class one day." He paused, trying to reconstruct the Greek myth in his mind.

"This story, too, is about the power of wishes. It begins in a stone hut in a faraway country called Greece, many years ago. An old farmer named Baucis had been married to his good wife, Philemon, for fifty-five years. Though they had very little money, they'd lived good and holy lives." Beloît rolled his eyes and yawned.

"One day the god of gods, Zeus, came down from his home in the clouds to visit the town where this couple lived. Disguised as a beggar, he went from home to home, asking for the small favor of food and lodging. He approached the wealthiest homes, but the merchants and bankers, the politicians and priests, all turned him away."

Beloît laughed and nodded. "That'd be just like rich folks."

"As night drew near," Pierre continued, "Zeus reached the poor farm of Baucis and Philemon. The great god, though he was dressed in tattered rags, received a warm greeting. 'You look weary, stranger,' Baucius said. 'You are welcome to a place by our fire, and a share of our modest supper.'

"'Thank you, good sir,' Zeus said. Philemon then offered the visitor a small bit of bread and cheese—all that they had in their larder—and invited him to spend the night. When Baucis apologized for their poor accommodations, Zeus said, 'You have offered all that you have. What more could a guest ask?'"

"The next morning Zeus revealed his true identity. 'I will return to Mount Olympus and punish your fellow villagers with a thunderbolt,' Zeus declared, 'but for your hospitality, old ones, I will grant whatever wish you request.'

"Baucis touched his wife's hand and smiled. 'Thank you for your generous offer,' he said. 'But we have everything we could ever want in this world—food and shelter, love, and the freedom to pray.'

"Zeus was amazed. 'But surely, there must be some small thing you could use—a palace, a bag of gold or jewels?'

"Philemon then whispered something to Baucis, and he smiled. 'Perhaps ...' Baucis began."

"'Go on,' Zeus prompted him.

"The wish the old couple made was that neither one of them should die before the other. 'If you could spare us, Great One,' Baucis requested, 'the agony of having to ever live alone, we would be forever grateful.'

"'It shall be done,' Zeus replied, shaking his head in wonder at the holiness he had found in this hut.

"A quarter of a century later the god's promise came true. It was a fine autumn day, and Baucis and Philemon had just celebrated their one hundred and first birthdays. They were walking through their olive orchard, when they paused to admire the setting sun. With their hands clasped and their faces set in satisfied smiles, a wondrous transformation took place. There was a clap of thunder high up in the pale sky. The ground trembled, and a cloud of smoke settled over the orchard. When the air cleared, Baucis and Philemon were no longer people, but two young trees, growing side by side, their roots and branches forever entwined."

Pierre glanced at Beloît, expecting a sneer, but he was surprised to see him squeeze Little Cat's hand and whisper something into her ear.

# Chapter Seventeen

# Making Ice

Deep winter days soon descended on the trading post, and the Ojibwe brought pelts to the storehouse nearly every day. La Petite taught Pierre how to tally the numbers and kinds of skins, and credit them to the correct family.

One afternoon La Petite ran his huge hands over a prime beaver blanket and said, "We were right when we guessed this was rich country. We'll have a full canoe to paddle back to Grand Portage in May."

At night the temperature dropped to ten or twenty below, and the lake boomed like a fusillade of cannons as the ice thickened. Sometimes the rumbling and cracking was so loud that Pierre had trouble falling asleep. A pressure ridge of ice in the middle of the bay piled up to the height of a man. "Those are tricky places," La Petite warned. "There could be open water out there no matter how cold the weather turns."

The thought of crossing bad ice worried Pierre, but he got the worst scare of all in his own bunk. After a long day of splitting and piling firewood with Louie, a pistol shot woke him in the night. "What's that?" he yelled, sitting up and banging his head on the upper bunk.

Beloît laughed as Pierre rubbed his aching head. Pierre was confused. No one had a gun and there was no powder smoke in the room either. "What on earth was that?" he asked.

"The logs," La Petite replied. "Go back to bed."

"Logs?"

"That's what I said," La Petite mumbled. Beloît was laughing so hard that it was hard to hear La Petite's sleepy voice. "When the green ones dry out, they crack. Especially on cold nights like this."

"That loud?"

"That loud. Go to sleep."

Pierre lay back, stunned by the power that had shot through the wall. He waited for another crack, but nothing came. He finally drifted back to sleep.

As the winter progressed, activity at the post picked up. Indian trappers regularly brought prime pelts from the neighboring villages of Wakemup and Nett Lake, and the voyageurs traveled by dogsled to trade with bands as far west as Pokegama and Big Sandy lakes.

To make up for the fish that had spoiled during the warm spell, André showed Pierre and Louie how to chop holes in the ice and set the nets under water. Three times a day the boys checked the nets, but the conditions were harsh and the catch small. To pull up each net, the boys had to chop the ice from the hole. Then they took off their mitts and plunged their hands into the icy water. "It feels like cold fire," Louie said. As they worked to untangle the fish from the net, they had to keep their hands in the water to keep them from freezing. One day after the boys caught only two small walleyes, André said "We'll have to put our netting on hold until spring." Louie and Pierre were not disappointed.

The winter jobs showed Pierre new sides of his crew.

André, the supposed dogsled expert, had promised to teach Pierre and Louie how to harness and run a dog team. But the boys soon discovered that he spent more time cursing the dogs than training them. He claimed that the dogs McHenry bought from the village were "unteachable" because they only understood "Indian talk." When a dog was lazy he'd yell *"Sacré chien mort"* (lousy dead dog) and crack his whip in the air. The dogs yelped at the sound of the rawhide snapping over their heads, but they only pulled half speed for the cook. However, whenever McHenry or La Petite took charge of the team, a simple *"Marche"* got the dogs running at full speed.

The voyageurs ran their dog teams with the same pride that they raced their canoes. Much teasing was dished out to a team that couldn't keep up. A slow sled was said to be "planted," and to escape that humiliation a man would push his five-hundred-pound load so that he and his team wouldn't get too far behind. Fatigue and frostbite were small pains compared with ridicule. Anyone who whined was dismissed with, "Wipe your own tears."

While André fought with his dogs, Augustine spent most of his winter days making furniture. Skilled in woodworking from what he called "whittling away idle time aboard ship," the old sailor showed himself to be a true craftsman. Working with just an axe, a draw knife, and an old file that he tempered in the fire, he made everything the men needed: tables, chairs, snowshoe frames, benches, sled runners, spoons, and bowls.

One afternoon after he'd carved a particularly fine bowl out of the swirly grain of a maple burl, he held it up with pride. "There's a shape hidden in every piece of wood, mate," he said to Pierre. "The trick is to let it surface." The scent of fresh maple lingered in the air, and Augustine was smiling in the soft light that filtered through the deerskin window. "It's a lot like loving a woman..." The old sailor whispered a name.

Pierre knew how a sudden loss could cut quick and deep. He wanted to know more about Augustine's life, but the sailor quickly changed the subject. "Would you look at that?" he said, holding up his index finger to show a spot of blood. "I've gone and cut myself."

During the winter the Ojibwe village was even busier than the trading post. The men spent their days hunting, trapping, and ice fishing. Red Loon showed Pierre how to spear fish through the ice by covering his head with a blanket and dangling a lure down the hole. At night they worked by the fire in their wigwams, fashioning tools and repairing equipment. The women sewed clothing, rabbit pelt robes, and moosehide moccasins that they decorated with beads and quills. They used birchbark to make baskets, cooking utensils, and food containers.

While Red Loon and the older Ojibwe boys hunted and trapped, the younger children played in the snow. They raced each other on snowshoes. They "snow coasted" down the hill above the village on slender lengths of wood. And they had contests throwing hooked sticks called snow snakes.

On Sundays Pierre often snowshoed to the village and watched the Ojibwe children at their games. One day Red Loon showed Pierre how to throw a  snow snake so that it cut into a snow drift and popped up on the far side. "When the snow is packed hard in the spring," Red Loon said, "we see how far we can skip these sticks across the top of the snow. A good throw goes farther than a strong man can shoot a bow."

Just then Beloît and Little Cat came by. Beloît's rabbit skin cap was now stained a dirty brown. The couple paused to watch the children skiing down the hill on curved bark slats that were only four inches wide. Beloît poked Little Cat in the ribs and said, "How about if I give it a try?"

Giggling as always, she agreed.

The children gathered to watch Father Bear make his first run. When a little boy offered Beloît a balancing pole to steady himself, Beloît brushed it aside. "I don't want nothin' slowin' me down," he declared.

Along with his capote, Beloît wore only leggings that left his thighs exposed to the cold. Pierre and most of the other men wore deerskin pants, but Beloît called them sissies. Pierre shivered as he watched the bare-legged bowman place one big moccasin on the ski and push off with his free foot. "*Je suis l'homme*," he yelled.

Pierre's eyes widened as the husky man hurtled down the hill. The track was icy from the many skis that had gone before him, and Beloît's extra weight made him fly twice as fast as any of the children had.

Red Loon asked, "Will he know enough to sit down?"

With his arms wheeling wildly and his free foot dancing on the snow, Beloît bellowed the whole way down the hill. As he shot onto the flat above the village, Little Cat called, "Stop, Jean. Stop, my darling."

Beloît was still traveling at top speed when he hit the first wigwam. Sheets of birchbark, bent poles, and blankets flew into the air as the shelter exploded. A yelping dog leaped out of the doorway, barely escaping with his life. Beloît never came out of the second wigwam. Little Cat found him lying dazed beside the smoldering fire pit. "My Jean," she called, falling to her knees.

By the time Pierre, Red Loon, and the curious children arrived, Beloît was on his feet. Though he was tipsy, he refused all help. "Tell the lady of the house that I'll pay for the damages," he told Little Cat, spitting a loose tooth from his mouth into the snow.

# Chapter Eighteen

# Holiday Bride

On Christmas Eve, McHenry invited Goodsky and his people to the post for a holiday celebration. A dozen Ojibwe families with children and babies crowded into the bunkhouse with the voyageurs on the evening of the party.

The smells of roast venison, beaver tail stew, and steamed wild rice mingled with the earthy scents of wood smoke, oiled moccasins, and wet blankets. The Ojibwe brought two drums and a wood flute to accompany Augustine's pipe. By the time the stew pot was bubbling in the fireplace, they'd formed an impromptu band and were playing a lively mix of native songs, jigs, reels, and folk songs. With the exception of Red Loon's uncle and Little Cat, the Ojibwe refused the rum. But the voyageurs toasted each other freely. And with every dram the noise in the room increased.

Pierre was used to a Christmas service of quiet hymns and candlelight back in Lachine. Though Father Michael smiled more broadly than usual on Christmas Eve, his conduct remained formal. Last year Pierre had spent more time studying Celeste than listening to Father's words. He recalled the moment she had stood for the benediction in her family pew at the head of the church. Her white shawl and bonnet had heightened the sheen of her black ringlets, as light danced off the frosty windows and filled the balsam-scented air.

As the voyageurs got wilder, the Ojibwe men and women paused in their dancing to stare. They were amazed at how fast the traders transformed themselves into stumbling fools.

But of all the fools, Beloît was the most obnoxious. "Let's hear that pipe, you weak-lunged landlubber," he bellowed at Augustine, as he spun Little Cat in a circle and lifted her into the air.

"Whew," he whispered to Pierre, "this one's a heavier load than a triple pack on an uphill portage." Then turning to Little Cat, he winked, "Ain't you, honey pot?" and kissed her plump cheek.

Beloît was dancing so wildly that in the middle of a leaping jig, he accidentally kicked André in the seat of his pants and sent him flying across the room. When André made a grab for the bowman, he tripped over a baby in a cradle board. The angry mother stomped toward André, but just before a fight broke out, Beloît settled it all by hugging both injured parties and convincing them to dance with each other.

Pierre was surprised when McHenry joined in the fun. After sharing some of his private stock of sherry with the men, he even tried his hand at dancing.

"*Mademoiselle*," he said, bowing elegantly to a pretty girl named Gageanakwad, or Clear Sky, who was Goodsky's eldest daughter, "would you care to take a turn?"

The men grinned as McHenry offered his arm to Clear Sky. The Commander then led the beautiful girl through the intricate steps of a fancy ballroom dance.

As the couple glided gracefully through the crowded

room, Goodsky beamed proudly. Later, when McHenry and Clear Sky retired to McHenry's quarters, Goodsky slapped Pierre on the shoulder and declared, "That's as fine a match as I ever could have hoped for."

Pierre frowned. It was hard for him to believe that Goodsky would be so accepting of his daughter's relationship. But the next morning he understood.

Pierre awoke to the sound of heavy snoring. The men were sleeping off the effects of their party. Pierre shivered. The bunkhouse was so cold that he could see his breath, and when he tried to lift his head, he was shocked to discover that his hair was frozen to the outside wall!

Trying not to yell from the pain, he gently pulled his stiff hair and blanket from the logs and looked around. Overnight the bunkhouse had been transformed into a crystal palace. Moisture from the steaming platters of food and the frantic dancers had crystallized on every surface. Overhead the log tie beams and ceiling were diamond flecked. Tiny rainbows glittered in the light from the windows.

As pretty as it was, Pierre was too cold to admire the scene for long. He needed to start a fire. He stepped outside to get some wood. The morning was blue and still. He smiled as he passed McHenry's cabin on his way to the woodpile. If he hadn't seen the commander's stylish dancing last night, he never would have believed it.

Pierre loaded his arms with wood. When he returned, the door to McHenry's cabin was partly open, and the commander stood there talking in a louder-than-normal voice. "I'd like to thank you for your company," he said, "but I'm sure you'll be wanting to get back to your family. Your father must be expecting you"—he pointed toward the village—"at home." McHenry stopped suddenly when he saw Pierre.

"Ah ... g-good morning, La Page," he stammered. Clear Sky waved to Pierre from inside. "I was just trying to explain to Clear Sky that ..."

"William McHenry," a voice boomed across the yard.

Pierre turned. Chief Goodsky was grinning. He had a blanket across his shoulders, but his head was bare.

"Hello, Goodsky," McHenry started. "I'm glad you've come. There's been a terrible misunderstanding. Though I've explained to Clear Sky that she's free to go home, either my Ojibwe is so poor or her French is ..."

"Her French is excellent," Goodsky said. "Though she can't speak it well, she understands nearly everything she hears. For certain she knows about marriage *à la facon du pays*." Pierre knew that meant "according to the custom of the country."

"But ..." McHenry stopped.

"I am honored, William McHenry," Goodsky said, "to welcome you into my family."

"Really, Chief," McHenry tried one last time, "this must be a misunderstanding."

Goodsky only smiled and extended his arms to embrace McHenry. "From this day forward you are my son."

# Chapter Nineteen

# Stalking the Long Shadows

The coldest weather of the season began the day after New Year's, when McHenry's thermometer registered fifty-three degrees below zero. The cold was so bitter that even the toughest voyageurs stayed close to the fire unless they needed to carry firewood or haul water. The sun didn't rise until after eight, and the sky was already dark by four in the afternoon.

One morning when Little Cat and Clear Sky were helping André serve breakfast, Beloît teased McHenry about his new wife. "It's sure nice to have a bunkmate to warm your bones in weather like this, eh, Commander?" he chuckled, giving Little Cat a squeeze.

Pierre blushed. McHenry looked ready to chastise Beloît. He pushed his bowl aside and touched his index finger to his temple, as if the bowman was giving him a headache, but then he smiled at Clear Sky.

"You're absolutely right, Jean," he said. Clear Sky smiled too. "Had I met a lovely lady like this two decades ago, it would have spared me many a lonely night on the frontier." Pierre knew that McHenry really cared for Clear

Sky, and he admired the commander for being honest about his feelings.

"Ain't that the truth," Beloît laughed. "I've never spent a winter in the north without a wife—I've had five grand ones over the years—and as long as I got my health and good looks, I don't intend to be alone."

His comment about good looks brought up a chorus of boos from the table. Augustine declared, "If it was good looks you were depending on, you'd have to shop for your wives at an almshouse for the blind."

When Pierre and Louie stepped outside to get an armload of firewood after breakfast, Pierre was startled by the bone-numbing cold. An instant chill penetrated his woolen capote and cap, making him shiver. Pierre sucked in a breath and his lungs burned. When he exhaled, his eyebrows and eyelashes frosted over. "I thought it was cold before Christmas," Pierre said.

"I never saw nothing like this," Louie nodded.

"You hear that?" Pierre looked down as his moccasins squeaked so loudly on the packed snow that he and Louie both laughed. They took turns stopping and starting, shifting their feet and grinning at the weird sounds. "It's like the ground is in pain," Louie said.

"You should see your head." The top of Louie's red wool cap was white with frost, and steam rose off his head and shoulders.

"You should see yourself," Louie said.

Feeling the cold creeping down his neck, Pierre said, "Let's get moving." With their shoulders hunched forward, they hurried toward the woodpile.

As Pierre bent to gather an armload of split birch, he saw a small icicle hanging from Louie's nose. "Your nose has grown, *Monsieur*," Pierre laughed so hard that he dropped a stick of firewood.

"Be careful who you pick on," Louie replied, pointing toward Pierre's face. Sheepishly Pierre wiped the back of his mitt across his own nose. The leather felt like tree bark against his skin.

The low was thirty-five below that night, and for the next two weeks the thermometer, even at mid-day, never rose above zero. The skies stayed clear and blue, but the sun had little power. The smoke from the chimney top dipped toward the ground instead of rising, and it trailed off in a thin, gray cloud across the lake.

To make matters worse, during the middle of the cold spell, Beloît had an accident with the bunkhouse door. Anxious to get to the outhouse one morning, he nudged the door with his shoulder. The leather hinges cracked in half, and the door fell into a snowbank. The men woke to a frigid blast of air. Cursing Beloît, Augustine leaped up from his bunk and propped the door back in place. Although Augustine made the final repairs during the warmest part of the day, it still took two hours of a blazing fire to warm the bunkhouse back above freezing.

When Pierre stepped outside at night, the stars were bigger and brighter than he'd ever seen them. Despite the cold, he often paused to study the constellation Orion. He imagined how ancient peoples must have stared at this same black winter sky and wondered at the bright-belted hunter.

When the cold spell finally broke, deep snows came. The first day after it rose above zero, a foot of fresh snow fell. And then it kept coming. Some days it was a light dusting; other days six or eight inches fell. By week's end there were four feet of new snow. This, added to the two feet that had fallen before Christmas, made woods travel difficult. The snow was so light and powdery that men on snowshoes sank to their knees.

Since the post was short of meat, McHenry dispatched hunting parties every day, but neither the Ojibwe nor the voyageurs came home with anything larger than a rabbit or a spruce hen.

One day Pierre's group returned with only three squirrels after an entire day in the woods. Over supper that night every man had his own explanation for the poor hunting. One blamed the moon, another said it was bad luck, but La Petite's made the most sense: "Game yards up after deep snows and doesn't move."

La Petite's logic didn't stop the complaining. The men grumbled over their meager portions of wild rice and squirrel meat. Pierre and Louie hooked a few walleyes on a hand line through the ice, but the fishing was as poor as the hunting.

"How can a man fill his belly on this?" Louie whined over his plateful of rice.

"Be thankful we still got rice," La Petite replied. "A few winters back I got so hungry that I chewed up my leather pack straps and was glad to have them."

When Louie looked at him doubtfully, the big man went on. "Anything is edible if you boil it long enough. A pinch of salt makes a sled dog harness or a moccasin top into a palatable stew. Ain't that right, Commander?"

The men turned toward McHenry. Though McHenry rarely spoke about his past exploits, everyone paid close attention whenever he told a story.

McHenry grinned at La Petite's tale. "It gets rough out there at times," he said. "I remember the first winter I spent on the Arctic Barrens. Traveling with the Chipewyan Indians, I ate the same things they did. If you get hungry enough, deer entrails, buffalo brains, even beaver fetuses are all palatable."

"Maybe this rice isn't so bad after all," Louie said, and the men laughed.

"But my favorite dish," McHenry continued, "was a lot like the haggis the Scots cook. It was half-chewed caribou meat, boiled in the animal's stomach and smoked over a fire. I acquired a real taste for that stuff. About the only thing I couldn't tolerate was raw bugs. Those Chipewyans used to gobble down lice like Christmas candy.

Louie paled at the mention of boiled caribou stomach, and even Beloît, who prided himself on what he called his cast iron guts, frowned at the description of eating lice. "I'd sooner..." he paused, searching for a fitting comparison.

"Sooner take a bath?" Augustine offered.

But Beloît shook his head, "I wouldn't go that far," he said, and the whole company chuckled again.

The voyageurs were so desperate for meat that McHenry sent the entire brigade out in pairs to scout for game. "The deer have got to be yarded up somewhere. Look for cedar thickets, spruce swamps—anywhere there's browse and shelter from the wind."

Since the Ojibwe were hunting, too, Red Loon and Pierre volunteered to go together. The evening before the hunt Red Loon invited Pierre to a ceremony in the Midewin lodge where Odinigan, who was a spiritual leader and healer, blessed their hunt. The men of the village began by blackening their faces with ashes and singing songs. Then Odinigan put sweet grass and herbs on the fire and waved the smoke over the hunters' clothing and guns. Finally he dipped his hand in red paint and touched the shoulder of each warrior.

The following morning Pierre and Red Loon put on their snowshoes and shouldered their muskets, shot bags, and powder horns. As they started down the packed trail, Pierre asked, "What do the ashes mean?"

"The men have vowed not to eat until we've found game. If our luck doesn't change soon, the children will go hungry. They might have starved already if my father hadn't made a trade for pemmican."

"Where would he get pemmican?" Pierre asked, recalling the berry and buffalo fat mix that was a staple of tribes further west.

"He traded McHenry's coat for two big packs," Red Loon

said.

Though the voyageurs were running short of food, it was worse for the Ojibwe, who had small children to worry about. Pierre admired Goodsky's generosity in giving up his elegant blue coat.

The boys silently followed the main trail which was packed from many hunters. Two miles from the village freshly broken trails branched east and west along the shore of the lake.

Pierre and Red Loon paused to study the two routes. "How about that ridge?" Pierre pointed toward a pine stand further west.

Red Loon didn't answer. He was facing due south, studying a barren tamarack swamp. Pierre frowned. "There won't be any deer out there."

With a slight smile, Red Loon turned. "Who says we have to hunt for deer?"

"What else would we..." Pierre stopped, recalling the bull moose they'd sighted near the Lost Lake Swamp last fall. The hawk's feather he'd found that day still hung in a pouch from his neck. "You're not thinking of going after moose?"

"If we want to fill the cooking pot," Red Loon said, "why waste our time on small game?"

Pierre grinned. "Lead the way."

An hour later Pierre regretted his words. The three-feet-deep drifts made it difficult to lift their snowshoe tips high enough to step forward. Though they took turns breaking the trail, by the time they'd crossed the swamp they were both exhausted.

The temperature was bitterly cold, but Pierre was sweating so heavily that he'd pulled off his woolen capote and tied it around his waist. Red Loon unlaced his heavy, deerskin shirt. As the steam rose off their shoulders, Red Loon joked, "We look as if we're ready to leap from a sweat lodge into the snow."

"Or as if..." Pierre stopped mid-sentence when Red Loon

suddenly raised his hand.

Pierre heard the sound too. Both boys raised their guns. The loud crackling of the brush was a sure sign there was a moose nearby. Though deer were usually silent in the woods, moose often charged ahead, trampling everything in their path.

A moment later the sound began to fade. Red Loon cursed and uncocked his gun.

"He must have caught our scent," Pierre said.

Red Loon nodded. "I'll bet he was bedded just ahead."

Only a hundred yards into the woods, the boys found a melted spot at the base of a balsam where the moose had been lying down. Pierre whistled softly when he saw the size of the bed. "He must be huge."

"I'll bet it's the big bull we saw last fall."

Fresh tracks led up the hillside. A deep trough between the hoofprints showed where the belly of the animal had dragged in the snow. In a brushy opening further on, older tracks crisscrossed in all directions. As far as the boys could see, the brush had been browsed off chest-high. "The moose have been eating breakfast, lunch, and dinner here," Pierre said, staring at bushes that looked like they'd been pruned flat by a gardener.

Red Loon studied the slope of the hill. "Since he was downwind of us, I'll bet he circles to the west. If we backtrack, we might cut him off."

"Let's go!"

The boys hustled through a low swale, where they paused to catch their breath. Red Loon pointed his musket toward a ridge. "That looks as good as any place." His blackened face was streaked with rivulets of sweat that gave him a wild look.

Keeping the wind in their faces, the boys sneaked through the pines and found a place that gave them a view of the opening below. Red Loon whispered, "This is perfect."

A half hour passed. Though Pierre pulled his capote

back on, he was chilled to the bone. His feet went from aching cold to numb. Just when he was ready to suggest trying somewhere else, Pierre heard the familiar crackling. Red Loon raised his hand to make sure his friend had heard. Pierre nodded.

A few minutes later, the moose appeared. Huge and dark, it was browsing casually, biting off alder twigs and chewing as it walked. If it wasn't the giant bull they'd seen last fall, it was his twin. Weaving back and forth through the brush, the moose drew closer to the boys. Pierre held his breath, hoping the wind wouldn't change and give them away.

Just before the animal walked within range of their guns, he stopped. With his head down, he kept eating and flicking his comically big ears.

Pierre was ready to draw back the hammer on his gun, when the moose laid down. "A nap?" Pierre whispered. He couldn't believe his eyes.

After a long while both boys were shivering with cold. Red Loon whispered to Pierre, "We have to risk a stalk."

Thinking of the hungry children back at the Ojibwe camp, Pierre agreed. Both boys started slowly down the hill. Keeping a big white pine between them and the moose, they crept forward. Once the moose lifted his head to sniff the air, and they froze.

When they finally reached the pine, Red Loon motioned for Pierre to sneak around the left side of the tree while he went to the right. As both boys stepped into the open and cocked their guns, Red Loon whispered, "Now."

Suddenly the moose stood up. It was a difficult shot, but Pierre aimed for the shoulder and squeezed. At the same instant a smoke plume issued from Red Loon's gun. The moose crashed into the snow.

The boys cheered. Red Loon jumped up to celebrate, but the toe of his snowshoe hooked on a buried branch, catapulting him into a snowbank. Pierre roared with laughter. Red Loon, his face smeared with snow and ashes, laughed too. When he tried to stand, his snowshoes crossed and he fell again.

Just then Pierre heard a loud snort. He looked up. The moose was on its feet and bolting for cover. "Hey!" he shouted. Pierre shook a measure of powder into his gun, but by the time he rammed a ball home and fired, the moose was out of range.

After Red Loon untangled himself, they examined the spot where the moose had fallen. Red Loon found a puddle of blood and a pile of whitish hair. "Gut shot." He shook his head, dismayed.

When Red Loon went to reload his gun, he couldn't find his shot bag. They searched where he had fallen and looked back along the trail, but there was no sign of it. Since Pierre had filled his pouch with mostly birdshot this morning, assuming they'd see more grouse and rabbits than deer, they were left with only a handful of musket balls.

"That's plenty if we shoot straight next time," Red Loon said, starting off on the trail of the wounded moose. The spots of blood in the snow made it easy to follow.

Neither boy expected to see the moose again so soon, but after they'd walked only two hundred yards, it jumped up and took off running through the thick brush. Red Loon took a hasty shot and missed. When Pierre fired, the animal went down. This time there were no cheers. Both boys reloaded quickly and started forward with their guns raised. When the animal leaped up again, they were ready. But this time the moose charged into a thick patch of willow, and both of their bullets were deflected.

Red Loon studied the place where the moose had fallen. "There's more blood, but I don't like how strong he's running." Pierre could see that the moose had taken huge jumps through the swamp.

A short while later, Red Loon became more confident. "Look," he said, waving his mitt at the fresh sign. "He's walking now. It won't be long before he beds down again."

A quarter of a mile further on, Red Loon whispered, "Get ready." He motioned toward a balsam thicket. Pierre checked his flint and raised his Northwest gun.

Red Loon stepped toward the trees. Pierre was expecting the moose to run out of the east side of the thicket, so he sighted on an open patch of ground just beyond the trees. To his surprise, the moose charged out of the balsams straight toward them. Pierre swung his gun and fired too quickly. He heard his ball whiz over the moose's head and thwack into a tree.

The moose turned, offering Red Loon a perfect shot, but when he pulled the trigger, there was a sickening click. By the time he dried his flint and recocked, the moose was running straight away. Red Loon shot and missed clean.

"Now we're done," Red Loon said. "That was our last ball."

"At least you aimed," Pierre said. "I shot way too fast."

Red Loon and Pierre studied the snow. The animal was badly wounded, but he could go for miles yet before he died.

"He's wolf bait now," Red Loon said, shaking his head. "What a shame."

The boys turned to head home. Pierre felt terrible. His feet were frozen blocks, and his heart was heavy. Not only would the children back at camp go hungry, but a proud animal was now in agony.

What would Robinson Crusoe do in a situation like this? he thought. "Wait a minute," Pierre said, pulling his knife from his belt. "I've got an idea."

Red Loon frowned. "You're going to run him down and stab him?"

Pierre shook his head. "No," Pierre slid the tip of his knife into the screw that held the trigger guard of his Northwest gun. He hoped he wouldn't break the blade, which his old friend La Londe had tempered with such care. A few turns later Pierre had a heavy brass screw in his hand.

"Do you really think it will work?" Red Loon asked.

"Our cook says that in an emergency you can load these muskets with anything–stones, marbles, or nails. So why not a screw?"

"It's worth a try," Red Loon agreed. "Besides, it shouldn't take much to bring him down now."

Pierre loaded his gun, and Red Loon led the way. After a half hour of careful stalking, Red Loon looked ahead. "I'll bet he's bedded up there." He pointed toward a hillside covered with young spruce. "I'll circle around. When he scents me, he's bound to come back down this trail."

As Red Loon worked his way quietly through the brush, Pierre positioned himself beside a big red pine. When he aimed, he would rest his gun against the side of the tree and take no chance of missing.

Just then he heard a loud crash. Instead of running south, the moose charged out of the trees, directly toward Red Loon. Though Red Loon yelled and waved his arms, trying to turn the animal toward Pierre, the bull kept running straight ahead.

Pierre tried to draw a bead on the animal, but he couldn't get a clear shot through the brush. He was ready to fire anyway, when he remembered a hunting tip from his father.

Knowing that he had only seconds to act, Pierre whistled. His first try was weak, but his second whistle pierced the air with a clear, high note.

The moose stopped and swung its head in Pierre's direction. Pierre aimed for his front shoulder and squeezed. The moose went down for good, and Red Loon and Pierre let out a loud cheer.

Pierre snowshoed over to the fallen giant. As much as the camp needed meat, it still hurt Pierre to watch the life ebb out of the great creature. Every hunt ended with the same green eyes—a "death glaze" his father had called it on the day four years earlier when Pierre had shot his first deer. He still wasn't used to it.

For Pierre hunting was a mix of joy and sadness. On one side was the need for food. On the other side was the right of wild creatures to run free. Pierre was confused whenever he tried to balance one against the other. As with so much of life, there was no simple answer, no clear right or wrong.

"We did it," Pierre spoke, whispering without meaning to.

"You did it," Red Loon replied. His voice sounded like his mind was far away.

"No, brother," Pierre insisted, "We did it. And to prove my point"—he paused with a wry smile and handed his knife to Red Loon—"the field dressing honors go to you."

"You shot it, you gut it, white man."

They both laughed softly, keeping their voices quiet out of respect.

Then Red Loon broke off a small aspen twig and placed it in a corner of the moose's mouth. He whispered a prayer to honor the spirit of the animal. Touching his finger to a drop of the moose's blood, he marked Pierre's forehead with a bright red streak. After he did the same to his own brow, he whispered, "From ashes to blood, the circle is now complete."

# Chapter Twenty

# Frostbite

"*Tu es l'homme!*"(You are the man!) Beloît cheered, slapping Pierre on the back, when he heard about the moose kill. The boys received a heros' welcome. It took a dozen men to pack the moose meat back to camp. The original plan was to divide the meat equally between the voyageurs and the Ojibwe, but when Pierre told Commander McHenry how short of food the band was, the voyageurs left the bulk of the meat for the village.

When Goodsky protested, McHenry insisted. "Just give us a few steaks," he said. "We've got a keg of pork fat left and plenty of rice." He turned to Louie. "We love rice, right?" he said, patting Louie on the back.

Though Pierre could tell that Louie was hungry enough to devour a hunk of raw moose meat, Louie smiled, "That's right, Commander."

"Thank you, gentlemen," Goodsky said. "We will hold a feast to honor your generosity and celebrate our good fortune."

The moment Pierre stepped inside the bunkhouse, he was struck by an incredible weariness. His cheeks felt flushed, and his feet, which had been numb all afternoon, suddenly began to burn. He sat down in front of the fireplace and bent to untie the frozen, knotted laces of his moccasins.

"Did your feet get cold?" McHenry asked.

"A little," Pierre nodded, struggling with the knots.

"How bad are they?"

"They're a little tingly now," Pierre admitted. "But I hardly felt them all day."

"We'd better take a look," McHenry said, borrowing a sheath knife from Beloît and cutting away the frozen laces.

As the commander pulled off Pierre's socks, the voyageurs crowded near the fire to have a look. Pierre felt silly with all the men gawking at his bare feet. "It's nothing," he insisted.

"We'll be the judge of that," the commander said.

Pierre looked at his feet. They were pale, and the big toe on his left foot was completely white.

"Looks like a touch of frost bite," Beloît said.

"Aye," McHenry agreed. "Would one of you boys fetch some warm water?"

In a short while Bellegarde returned to the bunkhouse with a bucket of warm water. The men were anxious to help. "We got to take care of the only decent hunter in the whole crew," Bellegarde said.

When McHenry lowered Pierre's foot into the water, Pierre bit his lip to keep from yelling. "That's hot!"

The commander looked worried. "It's barely lukewarm, son."

Two days later Pierre's foot was worse. His left toe had puffed up to twice its normal size and was turning black. When McHenry examined Pierre's foot that afternoon, he tried to distract Pierre with a story. "If you think it's cold around here, you should visit the Barrens sometime."

As McHenry probed his toe, Pierre's whole body

trembled. Since half the crew was watching, he tried not to flinch. "One day we cut down a dwarf spruce that was only eight feet high," McHenry continued, "but when we counted the growth rings, we found that little tree was three hundred years old. Further north, it's a vast arctic desert—totally flat with long stretches of muskeg. What little moisture falls can't drain through the frost. The sun never sets in midsummer. Millions of ducks and geese nest up there, and there's an explosion of wildflowers the like of which you'll not find anywhere else on earth." For a moment Pierre forgot his pain as he pictured this rare flowering.

"I already told you about the Chipewyan Indians up there. I was the first white man they'd ever seen." McHenry paused to grin. "They looked at me as if I'd just flown down from the moon. They stuck their fingers in my ears, nose, and mouth. They laughed at my blonde hair, which they said was as yellow as a pee-stained buffalo tail. They even pulled down my pants and giggled like little children when they found my whole body was the same pale color. When they finished, they declared me fit but 'weak-skinned.'"

Pierre laughed at the picture of the commander with his pants down. "So how's my foot?"

"To be honest, not good."

Pierre stared into McHenry's eyes. "How bad is it?"

"I'm sorry, lad. But before that poison spreads any further, we've got to take off your toe."

Pierre tried to fight back the tears. He thought of his father losing his thumb last year in a wood cutting accident. Pierre could still close his eyes and see the doctor sewing the skin flap over the stub. He could see the bloody bandage his father had bravely worn.

"Can't we wait just a little longer? Maybe it will..."

McHenry shook his head. "If it gets in your blood, you'll lose your foot ... or worse."

The pain in Pierre's toe was suddenly small compared to the cold clutch of fear in his stomach. "But what if it gets better?"

"There's no time to waste, La Page." McHenry had assumed his commander's voice now. It was clear he intended to proceed without delay.

McHenry turned to André. "Get some clean rags and ..."

But before he could finish, Beloît interrupted. "Excuse me, sir," he began. Every head turned toward him. Pierre had never heard Beloît say "excuse me" to anyone. "Little Cat fixed a boy in the village the other day who had an awful bad infection in his hand."

"We really don't have time to ..."

"Please, sir," Pierre asked, "can't we give it a try?"

"I can fetch her," Beloît said.

McHenry was clearly impatient to get on with his surgery, but he consented.

When Beloît returned with Little Cat, she carried a steaming pot that smelled like pine needles. "What's that?" Pierre asked, wrinkling up his nose at the gooey yellow paste.

"The inner bark of tamarack, plus a few secret ingredients," she said. Beloît winked at Little Cat and gave her a friendly pat as she stirred the mixture. She giggled as usual.

Though her laughter didn't make Pierre confident, he was happy to delay the amputation. When Little Cat pulled out her knife, Pierre frowned.

"We need to open the wound," she explained with a smile, "to help the salve work."

Pierre wondered if he'd made the right choice. If he needed to be cut open, perhaps McHenry would offer a steadier hand? But Little Cat had already heated her knife blade over the fire and was reaching for his swollen foot.

McHenry offered a distraction. "I never told you the strangest thing about those Chipewyans, Pierre. It was their medicine man. He had the usual spells and chants, but his specialty was stomach problems. One day he boiled up a big pot of lichen, pine bark, and reindeer moss tea."

"Yuck," Pierre said, clenching his teeth tight as he felt the first cut of Little Cat's blade.

"I tell you," McHenry continued, "it was remarkable the way that brew could clean out your system. One drink and you were running outside to drop your drawers."

As Little Cat's knife sliced deeper into his flesh, Pierre felt like he was going to throw up. Then everything went black.

When Pierre awoke, Little Cat was standing over him, smiling. His foot throbbed with a burning itchy feeling that made him want to scream. But when he looked down at his toe, its color was considerably better.

"What time is it?" Pierre asked.

"Nearly time for breakfast, you lazy pup." Beloît piped up from behind. Pierre couldn't believe that he'd slept through the night.

Pierre's foot ached for several days after Little Cat's treatment. But she applied the tamarack paste regularly until the ugly infection disappeared. McHenry was so impressed with Pierre's recovery that he gave Little Cat a present of a fine blanket and some ribbons.

# Chapter Twenty-one

# Sugar Bush

Red Loon swung open the door to the bunkhouse one morning in March. "Hey, Pierre, the crows are back," he announced.

"So?" Pierre said. He squinted in the bright light and yawned. It was just breakfast time, and he was still half asleep. He wondered why the arrival of crows would bring such excitement to Red Loon's eyes.

"That means the sap is running. My family is hiking up to our sugar bush, and Father says you can come with us if you like."

"When are you leaving?" Pierre asked.

"This morning," Red Loon said.

Pierre was still amazed at how quickly his Ojibwe friend made decisions. He never fretted over the details of plans and preparation. Back home Pierre's parents discussed things forever. It didn't matter whether it was a small thing like buying a second-hand plow or a big thing like his sister Camille's marriage. They talked the matter to death. To make matters worse, when it was all over they often worried that they'd made the wrong choice.

"Come if you can," Red Loon said. He was already on his way out the door.

"I'd have to ask the command..." Pierre started.

But McHenry, who was standing in the doorway, said, "We're still between seasons, Pierre. Take your holiday. Just make sure you bring us some fresh maple candy."

"That's right," Beloît spoke from a bench where he was whittling. "Some of us have got sweet tooths."

"There ain't nothing sweet about those rotten teeth of yours," La Petite called from the far corner. The rest of the men chuckled.

Beloît threw back his head and laughed, showing his tobacco-stained teeth. At least four or five were missing. "It's my lips, not my teeth, that the *mesdemoiselles* kiss. A man only needs a tooth or two to tear his meat—the rest are all extras."

Pierre gagged at the thought of anyone kissing Beloît's deformed face. He was suddenly glad to be leaving, no matter how short the notice might be.

Within the hour Pierre was tromping through the woods with Red Loon's extended family. Counting his aged grandfather and his young cousins, there were fifteen people. At first the frozen snow crust crunched loudly under their moccasins and toboggans, but by midmorning the sun had softened the trail. The only sounds to disturb the silence of the forest were the occasional bark of a dog or the squeal of a baby.

"How far is it?" Pierre asked Red Loon.

"About five miles. Just beyond that ridge where we took the moose last winter."

"Why don't you just tap those big maples on that ridge above the post?"

"Another family camps in that stand. We've traveled to this same maple grove since my grandmother was a small child."

"Do you always leave this suddenly?"

"My grandfather decides," Red Loon smiled. "Once he hears that first crow, he knows the weather is changing. It takes cold nights followed by sunny days to start the sap flowing."

For the next week Pierre lived with Red Loon's family in the sugar bush. The women and children tended the fires under huge moosehide vats of sap that bubbled day and night, while the men went hunting. Each evening the family feasted on roast venison or grouse or rabbit, while the sweet scents of sugar and maple-wood smoke hung in the air.

Mornings were magical in the maple stand. After waking to a frosty silence, Pierre heard the first far away plunk of a sap droplet landing in a birch bucket shortly after dawn. As the sun rose and the sap flow quickened, more drops plunked into the buckets that were hung across the ridge. The symphony continued until dusk when the cooling air slowed the stream of sap and brought the forest pulse to rest again.

Pierre could see why this was a special time for Red Loon's people. While the children played games, the old ones told stories about the sugar camps of years gone by. The nights were cold, but the days were bright and warm.

"The voice of the crow was true in predicting a fine sap run," Pierre said one evening as they sat before the fire.

Red Loon nodded and smiled. "The wild things teach us much when we are willing to listen."

# Chapter Twenty-two

# Last Testament

It happened on a perfect blue morning the week after Pierre returned from the sugar bush. Pierre was standing in the doorway of the bunkhouse, watching a smoke plume rise from the top of a distant wigwam. Beloît was outside, sitting on a log bench with his feet propped on a rum keg. Though he looked half asleep, the grizzled bowman suddenly sat up and pointed down the bay.

"It's time for a change of diet, *hivernant*," Beloît punched La Petite in the shoulder to get his attention.

"What did you have in mind?" the big man replied.

"Look." Beloît waved toward a pair mallards that were landing in an open patch of water between the island and the shore. The main part of the lake was still locked in ice, but the shoreline had begun to open in places.

"Ah." La Petite grinned. "Roast duck."

"I can taste it already," Beloît said, striding into the bunkhouse and taking his Northwest gun down from the wall where it had hung for the last month. "A finer fowling piece there never was than sweet Tillie," he kissed the brass dragon on the side plate of his rifle.

La Petite laughed and said, "If you treated your women as well as you take care of that gun, you'd have married a dozen wives by now."

"I've had plenty of wives, but this little beauty has brought down more meat than a whole brigade of women could."

Chuckling, Beloît slung his powder horn and shot bag over his shoulder. He clenched his gun barrel like a walking stick and stepped toward the door, tapping the butt plate on the threshold.

Pierre thought a cannon had gone off. He ducked his head and covered his ears.

When he looked up, powder smoke was billowing out of the doorway. As the haze cleared, Pierre was stunned to see that though Beloît was still standing, the left side of his face was completely gone. Blood was splattered over the log wall and on the ceiling and floor.

As they helped Beloît to a bunk, Pierre was amazed that the bowman remained conscious. La Petite tried to quiet him, but he insisted on talking. "It's lucky I shot myself in the left side, eh?" he joked, lifting a trembling hand toward the bloody hole that had been his cheek. "That way I didn't mess up the pretty half of my face. *Je suis l'homme.*"

"I'll get help," Pierre said, turning toward the door.

"No," Beloît groaned.

When Pierre stopped, Beloît's voice dropped to a whisper. "Come here, pup," he chuckled hoarsely. "There's not much time." Pierre stepped toward the bunk.

Though Beloît's breathing was labored and he was clearly in pain, he continued. "Since I got no kin, I want to leave you my year's salary."

"But why me?" Pierre stared.

"Apply the money to your schooling. Any of these rascals"– he waved his hand toward the men who were crowding through the doorway–"would waste it on whiskey and wenches. You got a chance to become someone."

Pierre was about to say more when the bowman motioned toward La Petite.

La Petite knelt to wipe away the blood that was running down Beloît's neck, but Beloît brushed his hand away. "I sure spoiled our duck hunt, didn't I?"

"Don't..."

"You see they bury me proper," Beloît cut in.

"You're not going to die."

"Spare me the lies." Beloît coughed. "I'm dead already." The big steersman leaned close to hear his raspy voice. Pierre missed his next words, but then Beloît spoke loudly enough for the whole room to hear. "When it's over, I want you to throw my carcass in a hole up in those red pines. Don't waste no burying clothes on me neither. I want to go out of this world the same way I came in— naked and ugly as sin." Beloît started to chuckle, but he coughed and gagged instead. The blanket beneath his head was soaked with blood.

By the time Beloît caught his breath, Little Cat had arrived with some bandages. But when she bent down to wrap the blue gingham across his face, he shook his head. "Save it for a kerchief," he whispered.

Little Cat sobbed softly as La Petite urged, "Just rest now," but Beloît continued.

"And I'll have no Bible thumping. If there's any preaching over me, I'll haunt every pipe stop and portage from here to Montréal." He grinned weakly.

"When it's all done"—he gulped a shallow breath— "don't be breaking a good paddle to make a cross. Plant me a tree."

Beloît fell into a fitful sleep. Throughout the day, Little Cat and Clear Sky took turns holding a cool rag to his feverish head. Little Cat sobbed the whole time.

"Hush woman," Beloît mumbled, but there was no stopping her tears.

As Pierre tried to comfort Little Cat, he thought how

strange it was for him to feel sorry for this man who'd ridiculed him for two years. Beloît's sudden generosity made Pierre wonder if he'd been hiding a gentler side all along.

However, if there was any real goodness in the bowman, he didn't let a hint of it show during his final moments on earth. Just when Beloît was struggling to draw in his last ragged breath, he opened one eye. Pierre jerked back from the sudden black sneer.

As weak as Beloît was, there was no mistaking his final words. "Stoke up the fire," he rasped. "I'm going straight to the devil."

Turning to Little Cat, he whispered, "Don't grieve, honey pot. You'll find yourself another fellow. A gal as pretty as you shouldn't never have to be lonesome."

Then, nodding toward the men who were gathered around, he said, "Keep your powder dry, boys."

Pierre waited for Beloît to take another gulp of air. Without realizing it, Pierre held his own breath, too. His heart pounded until his head felt light. Then he read the cold, unfocused stare in Beloît's eyes. It was done.

Little Cat let out a high-pitched wail and threw herself onto Beloît's chest.

Pierre stepped outside and drew in a deep breath. The twilight was heavy with the scent of dew. McHenry's "Sorry, lad," sounded far away, and he barely felt the gentle pat of Chief Goodsky's hand on his shoulder. Pierre walked numbly to the lake. He was a stranger, standing outside himself, even as he watched the dying sunlight above Daisy Island turn the horizon to pale fire.

Pierre had often wished beloit dead, but now that it had happened, he felt guilty. No one—not La Londe, not Kennewah, not even Beloît—deserved to be struck down in his prime. Death should only be for the old.

Pierre walked east along the beach, never stopping until he reached the edge of a cedar grove. He paused and looked up at a huge tree. Though its dark, spiraled trunk was already lost in shadow, the upper branches glowed with green gold light. Pierre couldn't help smiling when he recalled how often he'd come to this place to escape Beloît's mad cackling. But now that the fool was dead, Pierre knew he would miss him.

The next morning they dug a grave as Beloît had asked on the hill above the post, and they buried their bowman. Beloît's canoe mates carried his body up to the pine grove, followed by most of the Ojibwe band and Marie Antoinette, who appeared as if on schedule. The little bear had just crawled out of her den that week, and she wandered back and forth among the mourners, whining softly as she had on the day Beloît rescued her.

The grave was at the base of a huge red pine. Smelling of sweet loam, the earth reminded Pierre of the flower beds his mother would be planting back in Lachine about now. When they pulled the blanket off Beloît and lowered him into the grave, Pierre was shocked by the paleness of the bowman's skin. His naked body looked blindingly white against the dark soil. His chest was scarred from a knife fight, and his left shoulder was marked with the imprint of a large pair of teeth. Pierre wondered if the tooth marks were from the same man who'd bitten off half of Beloît's nose.

Little Cat, who had been wailing plaintively through most of the night, had painted Beloît's cheeks with two brown circles and drawn a finger-wide strip of vermilion through them. "The paint is to make him ready for the ghost dance in the northern sky," Red Loon whispered. "The food is to keep him from going hungry on his four days' journey to the hereafter."

With her own cheeks blackened to show her grief, Little Cat knelt at the edge of the grave and lowered a kettle of rice, a knife, and a tobacco pouch to Beloît's side. When she unsheathed a second knife, Pierre feared that she intended to do herself harm. But before he could step forward, Red Loon touched his arm. "It's all right," he whispered.

Pierre was relieved when she only sawed off her hair and dropped it into the grave. The coarse sound of the blade hacking off a handful of hair, accompanied as it was by the wailing of Little Cat and her family, sent chills up Pierre's spine. The bear nosed Little Cat's arm gently as she sobbed.

When Commander McHenry stepped forward, Bible in hand. La Petite said, "I'm sorry, sir."

"But surely a verse or two..." McHenry began.

"I gave him my word."

Pierre thought back to the Bible passage Commander John McKay had read when they buried Pierre's friend, La Londe: "Man that is born of woman is of few days, and full of trouble. He cometh forth like a flower, and is cut down: he fleeth also as a shadow and continueth not." At first Pierre regretted there would be no recitation today. But when he searched his mind for a verse that Beloît might like, he drew a blank. Perhaps silence was better than a sea shanty or a tavern song.

"It don't seem right," Louie mumbled, "to bury a fellow without so much as a single prayer."

La Petite turned to Pierre. "He asked you to throw in the first clod of dirt."

"What?" Pierre frowned.

"He said, 'Give that kid a fistful of dirt and let him dump it right on my face. Lord knows I deserve it after all the ribbing I gave him.'"

Numbly Pierre knelt and picked up a handful of damp earth. It smelled of pine needles and April wind. Pierre crumbled the black soil between his fingers and let it fall gently onto Beloît's pale chest. Pierre trembled as he stared at the cold body. It seemed as if he'd met this cackling fool only yesterday at the fur depot back in Lachine. And wasn't it only a moment ago that Beloît had been sitting on a rum keg in the sun?

A single misstep and a powder flash later, he had come to this. It was hard for Pierre to find any meaning in such random happenings. He wondered, is each day given to us as a gift to relish, or is life only a cruel trick waiting for the ancient woodland trickster, Winabojo, to show his hand?

The sound of yesterday's gunshot echoed in Pierre's head as he held his empty hand over the grave and watched the shadows of the pines play across Beloît's face.

After the men filled in the hole, La Petite took out a paddle, sharpened on the handle end. Using the flat side of a hatchet, he drove it into the ground at the head of the grave. On the blade he'd carved the initials JBB.

"He didn't want any crosses," La Petite explained, "but I figured we needed something to mark this little tree here." He knelt, scooped out a handful of dirt, and planted a white pine seedling. "Maybe one day this will grow tall enough to be a lob pine, one our grandsons can use to mark their journeys."

As La Petite patted the soil down, a little Ojibwe boy stepped forward and placed a piece of maple candy beside the seedling. La Petite said, "Thank you, son," then turned to the whole gathering. "The one thing Beloît did ask was that you all meet together back at the trading post, so I could make an announcement."

Pierre noticed strange expressions on the men's faces as they made their way back down the hill. Some looked like they'd been told half a joke and were waiting for the punch line. A few whispered about how strange it felt to bury a man that way. Most just shook their heads.

A short while later, the voyageurs and Ojibwe gathered outside the post to listen to La Petite. "Whether you liked Beloît or not," La Petite began, "we can all agree that he never pretended to be something he wasn't." Several heads nodded.

"I know we've barely had time to finish our breakfast,

and we've been to a burying and all, but Beloît wanted us to do one last thing. Since he was a heap more partial to celebrating than preaching, he asked if you gentlemen would empty a rum keg for him."

The men were stunned. They had expected a long-winded eulogy. For a moment no one moved. Augustine finally grinned when he realized that he'd been ordered to have a party. Throwing his hat into the air along with a half-dozen other men, he shouted, "To the memory of Jean-Baptiste Beloît."

# Chapter Twenty-three

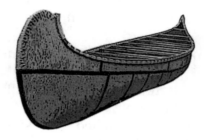

# Grand Portage Bound

That same night Pierre heard a far-off tinkling sound in the middle of the night, which meant the blackened ice sheet on Vermilion was breaking apart. At dawn he walked to the shore and was greeted by open, blue water and a pair of loons calling.

Later that week the brigade loaded up their furs and headed back to the Crane Lake post to reunite with the crewmen who'd wintered up on Quetico Lake. Along with the bundled furs, Pierre's canoe carried an extra bit of freight: McHenry's young wife, Clear Sky. Though some of the men were against bringing a native wife back east, McHenry was committed. "I've wandered enough years in the wilderness," he said. "It's time for me to settle down with this good woman and try my hand at another kind of work."

The day before the brigade left, Pierre and Louie stopped by the village and invited Red Loon to help them with a project.

"How would you like to help us with a little tree climbing?" Pierre asked.

Red Loon frowned. "What sort of tree did you have in mind?"

"We were thinking of a certain pine that stands next to Beloît's grave," Louie said.

"You know the one," Pierre got serious. "We thought about what La Petite said at the funeral when he planted that seedling."

"About it growing up to be a lob pine?" Red Loon recalled.

"That's right," Pierre said. "We figured it might be fun to have a lob tree here now."

Red Loon was suddenly excited. "I've seen those big lob pines that mark the main canoe routes up on La Croix."

"Don't you think it's time Lake Vermilion had its own marker?" Louie asked.

"I'll get my hatchet," Red Loon replied.

Two hours later the boys were scratched and sap covered, but they were satisfied. They had scaled the giant pine to within twenty feet of the great crown and lopped off every limb down to the middle of the tree.

They took a canoe from the village and paddled into Big Bay. The majestic pine, bare and tall, stretched a full twenty-five feet above the tree line. "You'll be able to see that thing from five miles away," Louie said in awe.

Red Loon and Pierre nodded and smiled in agreement.

Suddenly Red Loon frowned. "Didn't Beloît say he only wanted a little seedling for a grave marker?"

"That's right," Louie grinned.

"Besides," Pierre added, "when was the last time Beloît ever followed directions?" The boys had a good laugh as they paddled back to the village.

They kept the tree a secret until the day of their departure. As the voyageurs were loading the last of the fur bales into their canoes, Goodsky and Red Loon walked down to the shore to say goodbye.

With a grin Red Loon handed Pierre a canoe paddle.

"*Abwi*," Pierre smiled, remembering the Ojibwe name for a full-sized paddle.

Red Loon nodded. "My uncle made it especially for you.

He said, 'Pierre must not return home with a woman's paddle.'"

"Give your uncle my thanks," Pierre said, reaching into his pack and pulling out a red cap that he handed to Red Loon. "To keep you warm."

"I will think of you when the snows are deep," Red Loon said.

"One day I will return to Vermilion," Pierre said, embracing his friend one last time.

Chief Goodsky shook McHenry's hand and turned to Pierre. Touching the rawhide cord around Pierre's neck, the he said, "Remember your true name, White Hawk. No matter how far you may journey, the power of this place will go with you, and your *manitou* will protect you all the days of your life."

"Time to voyage, gentlemen," McHenry said, striding toward the waiting canoes.

When the canoes had pulled clear of the island and headed into open water, La Petite turned to have one last look at the fort.

"What the ..." the big man stopped.

Other heads turned. "Would you look at that," André declared. "A lob pine! Who on earth ever would have ...?"

By then Pierre and Louie were laughing. As the rest of the crew realized what they'd done, they all began laughing too.

"Ol' Beloît didn't want no fuss, but now he's got himself the biggest blessed grave marker this side of ..." André was stumped, trying to find the proper word.

"Let's be honest, gentlemen," McHenry said. "Shall we say the biggest marker this side of Hades."

With that they all had one last chuckle before they struck off for the north shore of Vermilion.

When McHenry's brigade arrived at Crane Lake, the first man from the Quetico group to greet them was Maurice Blondeau from the brigade that had wintered at Quetico. After shaking hands all around, Maurice asked,

"So where is that idiot, Beloît?"

When McHenry gave him the news, Maurice's first reaction was disbelief. The Quetico men realized it wasn't a joke, and everyone stood in awkward silence for a long time.

Pierre could understand their shock; Beloît had seemed indestructible. McHenry summed it up. "I would have wagered a year's pay that Beloît would have lived long enough to wear out many rocking chairs in his retirement."

After a quieter than normal bragging session that evening, the voyageurs retired early. Waking well before dawn, they loaded their pelts into the four north canoes and set off on the two-hundred-mile paddle to Grand Portage. Though the canoes were heavily laden, favorable winds helped the crew make good time. A steady breeze blew out of the west, allowing the men to put up make-shift sails, and they crossed the big water of Lac la Croix, Crooked, and Basswood in half the time it normally took.

When they reached Saganaga, Pierre was shocked to see that the south shore was still black from the previous summer's fire. "They say that the fire smoldered until the first snows," La Petite remarked as he surveyed the destruction.

In the low country, fresh shoots of ferns and wild grasses were brightening the understory, but the rocky ridges remained black and barren. Charred snags stood as grim reminders of the fire. Though the sun was bright and warm, the dead trees reminded Pierre of a winter day.

The voyageurs paddled the length of Saganaga in rare silence, staring at the dead land. Pierre winced as they paddled past their old campsite. He remembered the roaring wind, the thick smoke, and the death shriek of the squirrel that leaped flaming into the lake.

At the far end of Saganaga, just as the brigade was getting ready to portage into the Granite River, a young bear appeared at the edge of the water. Instead of running into the underbrush as Pierre expected, it stared curiously at the approaching canoes. The crew put down their paddles, and Maurice Blondeau pulled out a Northwest gun. Don't shoot, Pierre was ready to yell, but La Petite reached out with his long, steersman's paddle and tipped the gun barrel down.

"What in the blazes are you ..." Maurice stopped when he saw that every man in La Petite's canoe was staring at him.

The little bear stood his ground. Even as the canoes drifted closer, the bear tipped his head and studied the men intently.

Louie was the first to take off his cap, and in a moment, every man who had wintered on Vermilion followed suit. The men from the Quetico group stared at this odd salute. Pierre smiled. He was impressed that the brigade chose to pass up a chance for roast bear and honor the memory of Jean Beloît.

Only when the bow of La Petite's canoe touched the shore did the bear finally move. Even then he sauntered away slowly, turning twice to look at the men before he disappeared. "What a brave little fellow," Pierre whispered.

When Maurice asked, "What on earth is going on?" the men only smiled.

Pierre knew they would tell the whole story later that evening. He could see the canoe men standing by the fire and lifting their cups to toast Beloît. There would be many bold tales to tell, but for now it was good to listen to the silence of the forest.

# Pronunciation Guide for French Names
# and Other French Words

André Bellegarde (On-DRAY Bell-GARD)
Jean Beloît (ZHON Buh-LWA)
Maurice Blondeau (Mo-REECE Blon-DO)
Jacques Charbonneau (ZHAK Shar-bo-NO)
Augustine Delacroix (O-goos-TEEN Duh-la-KRWAH)
Joseph Jourdain (Zho-SEF Zhoor-DAYN)
Charles La Londe (SHARL La LOND)
Pierre La Page (Pee-AIR La PAHZH)
Joseph Le Petite (Zho-SEF Luh Pe-TEET)
Amblé Le Clair (Ahm-BLAY Luh CLARE)

à la facon du pays (a la fa-SON doo pah-YEE)
bonjour (bon-ZHURE)
Bastille (bass-TEEL)
capote (ca-POTE)
chanson (chan-SOHN)
en roulant ma boule roulant (ohn ROO-lohn ma boole
          Roo-lohn)
hivernant (ee-ver-NAHN)
hommes du nord (OM du NORD)
Je suis l'homme (zhu swee LOM)
La belle Lisette, chantait l'autre (La BELL lee-ZET,
          shan-TAY LOE-treh
madame (mah-DAHM)
mademoiselle (mad-mwa-ZELLE)
marche (marsh)
mesdemoiselles (may-duh-mwa-ZELL)
monsieur (muh-SYUR)
portage (por-TAZH; In English, POR-tej)
pose (poze)
rendezvous (ron-day-VOO)
sacré bleu (SACK-ray-BLUH)
sault (soo)
sacré chien mort (SACK-ray she-AHN MORT)
Vive Napoléon (VEEV na-po-lay-ON)
voyageur (voy-ah-ZHUR)

## Pronunciation Guide for Ojibwe Names
## and Other Ojibwe Words

Anishinaabe (a-ni-shi-NAH-bay)
Gageanakwad (Ga-GAY-a-na-kwad)
Gaazhagens (GAA-zha-GAYNS)
Kennewah (Ke-NAY-wah)
Kewatin (KAY-wah-tin)
Makwa (muh-kwa)
Odinigan (O-DIN-i-gahn)
Ojibwe (O-JI-bway)
Saganaga (SAH-gah-nah-gah)
Waawaashkeshi noondaa' gozigan (waa-waa-SHKAY-shee
                         noon-DAH go-zi-gun)
Winibojo (Wi-ni-BOO-zhoo)

abwi (a-BWI)
gashkadinogiizis (gahsh-kah-di-no-GEE-zis)
ikweabwi (i-KWAY-a-BWI)
manitou (ma-ni-TOO)
maanoomin (mah-NOO-min)
memengwe (may-mayn-GWAY)
midewin (mi-DAY-win)
nibowin (ni-bo-win)
wattape (wah-tah-PAY)

The Ojibwe language was exclusively an oral language until Europeans began to write it phonetically for documentation. Pronunciation, and so spelling, varies widely from region to region with no single version being right or wrong. We respectfully hope that no offense will be taken at the use of the language, as our intention is to portray the Anishinaabe culture more vividly through including Anishinaabemowin.

# If you enjoyed this book, you may also like these

*Midwest Book Awards*
**Honorable Mention
History**

## *A Wonderful Country*
### *The Quetico-Superior Stories of Bill Magie*

Bill was a guide in his young years and after retirement. He was an engineer on the first surveys of the Minnesota-Ontario border, and he spent years living in the Canoe Country in all seasons and with all kinds of people, from CCC camp workers to wealthy clients to Indians and loggers and trappers. Reading this book is like sitting around a campfire listening to an oldtimer. Bob Cary reminds the reader, "Do not be concerned if you have a difficult time trying to separate fact from fiction. Bill Magie never intended that you should." From Saganaga to Lac LaCroix and Atikokan to Ely, Bill tells stories from the places Boundary Waters travelers know well.

*The irascible Bill Magie offers today's Canoe Country travelers an invaluable and entertaining glimpse into the wilderness of bygone days. Reading Bill's stories makes you wish you could have shared a campfire with him 70 years ago. Thanks to Dave Olesen, you almost can.* – Sam Cook, author of *Up North* and *Camp Sights*

## Both books are available at
## www.ravenwords.com and your local bookstores.

# Raven Productions books for young adults –

**WINNER!**

*The Lupine Award*

*Moonbeam Award*

*Midwest Book Award*

*Independent Publishers Award*

Kristin's Wilderness
A BRAIDED TRAIL

## Kristin's Wilderness
### A Braided Trail

This artistically created book tells the story of a young girl growing up among wildlife researchers in the northwoods. She finds her way into womanhood through the important relationships in her life, including the old Finnish ladies who share the sauna, two wolverines escaped from their observation pen, and the northern native people with whom she spends a winter. Generously illustrated with delicate watercolors, the story is beautiful and gentle, yet it will move you to tears and make you grin.

*I can't say enough how much **Kristin's Wilderness** touched us. While we look at many books each year, it is not often that one gets the sense as soon as it is taken from the box that it is something very special. **Kristin's Wilderness** is the most remarkable book that I have read since being on the committee.* Connie Cushing, chairwoman of the Lupine Committee

*Kristin's Wilderness is a wondrous chapter book for readers aged eight to eighty ... The paintings especially capture the mood and majesty of the natural world ... in this gentle and heartwarming tribute to coming of age.*
Midwest Book Review

# About the Author

William Durbin is an author and a former teacher who lives on Lake Vermilion at the edge of Minnesota's Boundary Waters Canoe Area Wilderness. Durbin's interest in the voyageur period dates back to his junior high school years when he took his first canoe trips in the Boundary Waters and Quetico Provincial Park. In those days he loved to imagine what it must have been like for the fur traders two centuries earlier, paddling and portaging their birchbark canoes through a vast network of rivers and lakes rimmed with stands of virgin pine. Thirty years later Durbin turned his love of canoeing into two novels, *Wintering* and *The Broken Blade*. These books combine his knowledge of the outdoors with factual information gleaned from the classic journals of the fur trade period—those written by Daniel Harmon, Alexander Henry, David Thompson, Alexander Mackenzie, and others.

A winner of the Great Lakes Book Award and a two-time winner of the Minnesota Book Award, Mr. Durbin has published ten novels for young readers. In addition to *Wintering* and *The Broken Blade*, Durbin has written *Song of Sampo Lake*, *Blackwater Ben*, *The Darkest Evening*, and three books in Scholastic's "My Name Is America" series: *The Journal of Sean Sullivan*, *The Journal of Otto Peltonen*, and *The Journal of C.J. Jackson*. His most recent work, *The Winter War*, deals with Stalin's invasion of Finland in 1939. Jane Startz Productions (*Tuck Everlasting*, *Ella Enchanted*) is currently working on a film version of Durbin's award-winning novel, *El Lector*.